ARKSPUR HOUSE

Dear Friend,

You ~~HAVE TO COME HELP US~~ are cordially invited to a house ~~THAT WANTS TO SCARE YOU~~ unlike any you've ever entered—one that understands your wishes and dreams, and wants to ~~KEEP YOU FOREVER~~ help make them come true.

Few have been called ~~AND EVEN FEWER ESCAPE,~~ but if you're reading this, you're one of the Special ones. Come. Let's play.

Most sincerely,

~~Larkspur~~ *SHADOW HOUSE*

Enter Shadow House . . . if you dare.

1. Get the FREE Shadow House app for your phone or tablet.
2. Each image in the book reveals a ghost story in the app.
3. Step into ghost stories, where the choices you make determine your fate.

 For tablet or phone.

scholastic.com/shadowhouse

SHADOW HOUSE

You Can't Hide

SHADOW HOUSE

You Can't Hide

DAN POBLOCKI

SCHOLASTIC INC.

Library of Congress Control Number Available

ISBN 978-0-545-92551-8

10 9 8 7 6 5 4 3 2 1   17 18 19 20

First edition, January 2017

Printed in China 62

Scholastic US: 557 Broadway • New York, NY 10012
Scholastic Canada: 604 King Street West • Toronto, ON M5V 1E1
Scholastic New Zealand Limited: Private Bag 94407 • Greenmount, Manukau 2141
Scholastic UK Ltd.: Euston House • 24 Eversholt Street • London NW1 1DB

For Maria

CHAPTER 1

DYLAN RAN, HIS thoughts and memories as blurred as the shadows that kept pace with him. His twin brother's voice rang out behind him, but it only made him run faster. He ran, choked with fear, desperate to escape everything he'd just been through.

Although, in a way, he hadn't been through anything.

Dylan was dead.

He skidded around a corner and slipped on the runner that had suddenly appeared in this stretch of hallway, pinwheeling his arms to try to stop but slamming into a wall anyway. That was Larkspur House for you, changing with no warning, and always trying to trip you up. There was no getting used to this nightmare.

1

Dylan leaned against the door, panting from his sprint, and put a hand to his chest. His heart pounded against his palm, and his pulse fluttered in his neck. His cheeks were hot, and he wiped sweat from his forehead with the side of his arm. He felt real. He felt alive.

Only now he remembered—the prank his twin brother, Dash, had played on him. Dash's face lit up with glee, and then a split second later contorted in a scream. The blast of white, the blood in his mouth, pain everywhere. Stillness. He gave himself a shake, as if he could chase it all away.

But he couldn't. No one can chase away death; death chases *you*.

Somewhere deep in his mind, a thought wriggled like a worm. Had Dash meant to do it? His brother had always been the good twin, his mother's little angel, and the pet of every director they'd worked with over the years in LA. Dylan was the bad one, the hassle. The reason the scripts stopped coming. Did some part of Dash want Dylan gone?

Dylan closed his eyes. He missed LA—he'd give anything to go home, to get away from this haunted place.

He laughed, and the sound crackled down the corridor. *He* was one of the ghosts haunting Larkspur now.

Dylan forced himself to open his eyes and look around.

He was in a hallway he hadn't seen before. The wooden floor and paneled walls were nearly black. A dim glow came from above, and he could see the ceiling was angled like a rib cage. A latch clicked, and somewhere a door opened.

He shrank from the sound of squeaking hinges and hunched his shoulders as if he could make himself disappear. *But couldn't he?* He was dead, after all.

Footsteps echoed into the hallway, and a tall silhouette disturbed the glow up ahead. Dylan pressed himself against the nearest wall. But the stranger approached quickly—too quickly for Dylan to hide.

A familiar tingle settled onto his scalp, like a cap made of needles, and Dylan watched as the hallway tilted.

Flash.

The dressing room. The bucket of water above the door, a classic trick.

Flash.

Cold, wet, reaching for the lamp. The shock, the blinding white. Electrocution.

Flash.

The funeral.

Flash.

Dash's room in the psychiatric hospital.

Flash.

Flash.

Flash.

A voice called out to him, but he couldn't stop himself from crumbling to the ground. And then everything went black.

"Dylan?" someone said from the darkness. "Dylan?"

Dylan's eyelids fluttered open. He was lying down. There was a wooden ceiling above him and a plush carpet beneath him. Sitting beside him was a man he'd never seen before. The silhouette from the hallway? He was broad-shouldered and had a bushy beard, and wore a red-and-black plaid shirt and dark-blue jeans. He looked like he might be a lumberjack, or at least someone who lived in one of the cool neighborhoods in LA. The man's hand rested on Dylan's shoulder. Dark hair hung just past his thick eyebrows, slightly obscuring his glistening, golden-hued eyes. "Are you all right?" he asked.

"I-I don't know," Dylan answered. "What happened?"

"We were running your lines and you fainted. Your eyes rolled back and then, *blam!* You hit the floor."

"My lines?"

"Man, you must have really smacked your head hard. My assistant is getting some water for you. She'll be back shortly.

Just rest." Dylan tried to wiggle out from under the man's hand, but it was wide and heavy. "Don't move. You'll be fine."

"What *lines* are you talking about?" Dylan asked, shivering, worried that his voice was rising, revealing his alarm. "Who are you again?"

The man smiled, then seemed to catch himself, furrowing his brow. He unbuttoned his plaid shirt, revealing a white T-shirt underneath. He slipped the plaid shirt off, draping it over Dylan like a blanket. "Del Larkspur? I'm the producer of *The Gathering*. You're one of my leads. The big bad villain." He paused, examining Dylan's confused expression. "You're here, with your brother, shooting a horror movie. Do I need to go on?"

"*The Gathering*?"

Del ran his hand through his hair as if trying to hide growing frustration.

Dylan felt a hole open in his mind, sucking away memories of what must have been a horrible dream. *A dream that had felt entirely real.*

A neat pile of papers was on the rug to his left. It looked like a script. At the top of the opened page, the name of a character was written in black pen: *The Trickster*. "The film," he said. "Of course." Some details were starting to come back. There were creepy masks. And ghosts. And a great big mansion to play in. But wait, it wasn't a movie. It was real. He'd just found out he was . . . Dylan's brain refused to go on.

"We met you this morning?" Dylan asked. Del nodded. "And Dash is . . . *where*?"

"With the director, Cyrus Caldwell," said Del. "They're finishing prep with the other kids in the cast for the big shoot tonight."

"Can I see my brother?"

"Why?"

"I-I just want to ask him some questions."

Still squatting by Dylan's side, Del rocked back on his heels. The lines around his mouth tightened. "I thought you two were doing your own things here. Separate roles now. Wasn't that what you wanted?"

Dylan sat up fully. Crowded bookshelves filled the walls. A fire was burning in a fireplace, flicking orange light into the room's nooks and crevices. "You're right," he said quickly, not wanting to annoy the man any further. "I'll catch up with Dash after the shoot."

"Good," said Del, warmth returning to his face. "I really need you with me on this. Put on that shirt. It can get drafty in here."

Del's smile made Dylan feel happy. Like he was wanted.

Appreciated. The bad dream was fading, and relief heated Dylan's veins. Dylan inhaled a deep breath. He slipped his arms into the sleeves of Del's button-down and then grabbed the script from the floor, holding it in his lap, plucking at the brass clips that bound the pages together. "I'm sorry," said Dylan. "I'm not sure what happened to me before, with the fainting and all that, but you can count on me. I promise."

"Good," said Del, standing and heading toward the fireplace. "Because I wouldn't want to have to replace you." Dylan felt the blood drain from his cheeks. Del went on, "I've got something else that'll help you get back into character." He grabbed an object from the mantel. "It came from the props department." Turning, Del held it out. It was a face.

A mask.

Wide, empty holes stared up at Dylan. Exaggerated eyebrows arched in pointed peaks. A bulbous red nose protruded from the center of the face, and ruby lips were smeared in a sad frown. Painted tears tumbled down the cheeks.

Dylan's stomach writhed as he took the mask from Del. "This is who I'm supposed to be?" he asked. "A clown?"

Del nodded, his amber eyes gleaming in the fire. "Put on that mask, and you'll know exactly what I need you to do."

Dylan's pulse beat a warning, but he slipped the strap over his head. The mask hugged his face tightly. He'd expected it would be difficult to see through the eyeholes, but to his surprise, for the first time since waking from his faint, he could see everything clearly.

"Our *Trickster*," Del whispered, his tone somehow deeper now, raspy. "It's time to get to work."

CHAPTER 2

"DYLAN! WAIT FOR us!" Dash called out to his brother. He swung his phone light back and forth frantically, illuminating the hallway.

"Dash, slow down," said Poppy, reaching for his shoulder. "We could be missing clues."

He shoved her hand away. "Clues? What do you think this is, a detective movie?"

His sneer made Poppy cringe. "M-maybe his sneakers scuffed the rug. Or . . . or . . ."

Dash turned back to the tunnel of shadow that was the hallway. "DYLAN!" he yelled as he plunged ahead.

"Good job," said Marcus, "since the louder you are, the more invisible we become to every creepy thing in this house."

"It doesn't matter," said Dash. "I have to find my brother!"

Azumi ran up ahead of the others and grabbed Dash. "You and Dylan aren't the only ones who need help. We're *all* trapped in this freaky house. We've got to work together if we want to get out."

"Fine!" Dash shouted. "Let's work together, then. Help me find Dylan!"

"I wish you wouldn't speak like that." Azumi kept her voice even. "None of us deserves it." She touched Poppy's arm. "Besides, you know that Poppy can be a little . . ." She raised an eyebrow.

Poppy pulled away from her. "A little *what*?"

"A little sensitive," said Azumi.

Poppy flushed. As if to prove how wrong Azumi was, she grabbed Dash's hand. He cringed but she held tight. "You want help? Here." Directing his phone's flashlight at the floor, she said, "Check the rug for scuff marks. Slow down and listen for doors or footsteps or other sounds. *Observe*. That's how we'll find Dylan. But mostly, remember to breathe."

Dash glared at her. "Can I have my hand back, please?"

Poppy let go abruptly and stepped away from him.

The kids came to a T-shaped intersection and Dash paused to examine the Persian rug. "It looks like there might be footprints heading this way," he said quietly, not looking at Poppy.

"But we don't know who left them," said Marcus. "What if it's the ghosts in masks again? The Specials? What if they're hiding somewhere, watching us?"

Poppy forced a smile. "Then we pull off their masks and we handle them. We know what to do now. It's best to stay positive so we can find Dash's brother and get out of this place."

"I can hear you, you know," said Dash, his voice flat.

"That's okay," said Poppy, her cheeks flashing red again. "We're not hiding anything from anyone anymore," she added.

Marcus glanced at her. "Was that a jab?"

Feeling suddenly brave, Poppy met his gaze. "If it was a jab," Poppy went on, "I think I'd have a right to make it." Back at Thursday's Hope—the group home where she'd spent most of her life—she would never have stood up to the girls like this.

"We're all on the same side *now*," said Azumi, stepping between them. "Aren't we?"

Marcus sniffed and turned away. He felt naked without the music that usually ran through his head. The house had twisted the music, broken it. But it wasn't gone for good. *Was it?*

11

"Shh," said Dash, stopping suddenly several yards ahead of them. "Listen."

"What is it?" asked Marcus.

Dash held up a hand. The others gathered around him. A soft thrumming filled the air.

"Maybe it's a clock?" Azumi suggested.

Dash shook his head. "Sounds more like a heartbeat."

"That's one loud heartbeat," said Marcus. "Where's it coming from?"

"Look," Azumi whispered, pointing at the wallpaper. It was a deep, iridescent blue layered with a Gothic design in black velvet that looked like poisonous vines crawling up an iron fence. The vines were pulsing slightly, as if blood were rushing through them.

"So sick," said Poppy.

"Is this real?" asked Marcus.

"It's another trick," Dash said, pulling his flashlight away. "To keep us from looking for my brother."

"Don't touch it," said Marcus, grabbing Azumi's hand away just as she made contact. Azumi yelped and put the tip of her finger into her mouth.

"Are you hurt?" Marcus asked her, reaching for her hand again.

Azumi shook her head. "Static electricity," she said.

"Dylan!" Dash called out again, moving farther into the darkness.

Following Poppy and Dash down the blue hallway, Marcus noticed Azumi was rubbing her finger. "You sure you're not hurt?" he asked.

Azumi half glanced at him. "It's nothing."

"Maybe Poppy has another Band-Aid in her magic pink messenger bag," said Marcus.

Before he could ask, Poppy called back to them, "Dash found more scuff marks on the rug. They lead to a door!"

CHAPTER 3

POPPY AND DASH stepped cautiously into a long room.

Six iron beds were lined up against each wall, their feet facing the center of the room, where a long aisle divided the two rows. Each mattress was made up with a dusty white sheet, the corners tucked in military style. At the far end of the room, three wide windows allowed daylight inside, although shadows lurked between the beds. A pane in the left window was cracked and held together with masking tape. Beside the windows, two closed doors on opposite walls faced the center aisle.

"Whoa," said Marcus, coming up behind them. "What is this place?"

"A dormitory," said Poppy, tight-lipped. She used to sleep in one just like it. "It's where the orphans must have lived."

"Windows," said Dash with relief, racing toward the other side of the room. He grabbed for the sash panels, but they were wedged shut.

"Pull the tape off," said Poppy. "Maybe that crack weakened the glass. Maybe *this* one will finally break and we can get out of here."

Dash worked the tape under his short fingernails. But when he yanked the brittle tape away—*zip!*—the crack oozed together and sealed itself. "What the . . . ?"

Azumi approached, peering at the drop outside the window. "We're too high up anyway."

"We could tie all the sheets together," said Poppy. "Make a rope. We could—"

"None of it matters if we still can't smash through the glass," said Dash. "Besides, we've got to keep looking for my brother." He waved the group back toward the main door. "I guess those marks on the rug didn't mean as much as we thought they did. Let's go."

"Dash, can we rest for a bit?" asked Azumi.

"*Rest?*"

"I can't be the only one who's totally wiped out."

15

"I wouldn't be able to rest if you paid me a billion dollars," said Poppy.

"What about a *trillion*?" asked Marcus with a tired grin. When no one laughed, he cleared his throat and went on. "Maybe Azumi's right. We've been moving full throttle since early this morning. Dylan's not going anywhere."

"How do you know where he's going?" asked Dash. "Those orphans—those *ghosts*—might have found him already. They might be looking for *us* again at this point. We can't just lie down in their old bedroom and wait for them to come shambling along."

Azumi slumped and gripped the closest bed frame.

"You two go do what you want," said Marcus to Dash and Poppy. "I'll stay here with Azumi. Meet us when you're ready."

"When we're ready?" Dash echoed, his voice low. "You mean, like, when we find my *brother's ghost*? After that, everything will be just peachy keen?"

Marcus blushed. "You guys keep twisting my words."

Poppy looked pleadingly toward Azumi, who sat on one of the mattresses and hung her head. "We shouldn't split up—"

"She's not feeling well!" Marcus interrupted. Azumi let go of her finger and shot him a glance. "And neither am I. I'm dizzy and shaky. I bet you guys are too, but you're just too stubborn to admit—"

The light dimmed as the sun was devoured by a passing cloud, and a soft knocking came from across the room. Two dark figures stood in the doorway: a man and a woman, their features hidden by shadow.

Everyone froze. Azumi instinctively slid against the bed's headboard and pulled her knees up to her chin.

The man's fist was raised, his knuckles resting on the wood frame.

"Excuse us," said the woman. Her voice had a silky southern twang.

"Are you *actual* adults?" Marcus asked, still stunned.

"Marcus!" Azumi said through a clenched jaw, her eyebrows pitched.

The woman laughed as if surprised by Marcus's boldness. "You probably don't see too many adults around here."

"Can you help us?" said Marcus, stepping toward them tentatively.

"That's why we're here," said the woman. "To help."

Poppy's heart fluttered with hope. She pinched her arm, not trusting her eyes and ears. "What do you mean, 'That's why we're here?'" she asked. "How did you know we needed help?"

"We have an appointment with Cyrus Caldwell," said the man. "But we seem to have gotten lost in this monster of a building, and I'm afraid we must have missed him."

Poppy took a slow step back, closer to Marcus. Her skin prickled with dread. "Cyrus Caldwell. We read about him in those files we found," she whispered. "The director of the orphanage. The one who died decades ago."

Dash backed toward where Azumi was crouched on the bed.

"Can you tell us where we might find him?" the woman called, her teeth gleaming from the shadows as she grinned.

The couple stepped into the room, and the daylight dimmed even further. The man wore a charcoal-gray suit. His dark tie was attached to his white shirt with a gold pin in the center of his chest. His hair was slicked into a part, like someone Poppy had once seen in an old television show. The woman was shorter than him, but in her bright-red wool dress she looked almost as large. Delicate white pearls hung from her ears, and a wide-brimmed white hat seemed to float like a halo over her head. There was something familiar about these people. They had a half-hopeful, half-desperate air around them that reminded Poppy of a couple searching for *family*.

"Oh, you poor dears!" said the woman, as the children continued to back slowly away. "We must have frightened you so, bursting in like popping balloons! *Pop-pop-pop!* You mustn't have very many visitors here at Larkspur."

"You'd be surprised," Dash murmured.

"We are Mr. and Mrs. Fox," said the man. "Foxes in the henhouse! Ha-ha!" He turned to his wife and smiled.

"You can really get us out of here?" asked Marcus.

"Marcus!" said Poppy, peering at him from the corner of her eye. "Shh. They think they're going to adopt us."

"Adopt us?"

"Well, of course we are, silly heads," said Mrs. Fox, looking directly at Poppy. "Isn't that what you've always wanted, Poppy? Parents? A family?"

The question hit Poppy square in the chest, nearly knocking her breath away.

"How do you know her name?" asked Dash, turning to Poppy and glaring, as if *she'd* said something wrong.

"Oh, we know all about little miss Poppy," said the woman. "On the phone, it was quite clear that Mr. Caldwell just adores her."

Poppy began to tremble. "B-but I've never met him!"

"Are you sure about that?" asked the man, grinning

strangely. Holding hands, Mr. and Mrs. Fox stepped into the aisle between the two rows of beds.

"Stop!" said Dash, holding up his hands. "Don't come any closer."

But they ignored him. "We only have to finalize everything with Mr. Caldwell, and then it will be settled," said Mr. Fox. They took another step, the dusky light from the window finally revealing their faces. "What do you say . . . Poppy?"

Poppy covered her mouth to hold in a scream.

CHAPTER 4

THE FOXES' SKIN was waxy and drawn. Their lips were sunken, their eyes hooded with darkness. Mrs. Fox opened her mouth, and a line of spittle pooled over her chin before dripping onto her red dress. "What's wrong, dear?" she asked. "You look ill." She pulled off her gloves, exposing withered, skeletal fingers. She reached toward Poppy, her ruby nails like claws. "Let me feel your forehead, dear. You might have a fever."

"No!" Poppy yelled. "Don't come near me!"

Mr. Fox put on his hat. His cracked lips deepened into an unnatural frown. "Cyrus mentioned that your birth mother couldn't wait to get rid of you. I'm starting to see why."

Poppy's cheeks burned as if he'd slapped her face. "Cyrus doesn't know anything about me! And neither do you!"

"Coming with us would be better than what you have now." Mrs. Fox smiled. "A great big fat *nothing*. A huge pile of *no one* . . ." Drool spilled out of her mouth again. She used one of her gloves to dab daintily at her chin and neck, missing most of the liquid. "Home take. We'll . . ." She drifted off for a moment. "Then you'll see. Different be . . . There . . ."

"Home, yes," said Mr. Fox, edging forward. "China dolls . . . Canopy beds . . . Chores, of course, but what home . . . isn't home without . . . a little bit of work?"

The Foxes were almost halfway up the aisle now.

"You're not real!" Poppy shouted out. "You're . . . you're just his puppets! Cyrus is going to have to try harder if he wants to break us!"

Azumi's face went red. "Poppy! You'll make them angry!"

The Foxes released a gritty sound from their chests, something animal and dangerous. The noise was terrifying, but somehow it also made Poppy glad, as if she'd struck a blow.

Her gaze fell upon the doorway behind Azumi and Dash. Another door was only several feet from where she and Marcus stood—an escape route! She bent down and grasped the frame

23

of the bed in front of her. "Flip these up!" she yelled. Together, she and Marcus lifted the bed onto its side.

The mattress fell to the floor with a satisfying slump, and the metal frame stood like a barricade separating them from the phantoms. The Foxes quickened their pace.

"Hurry!" Poppy shouted to Azumi and Dash, who flipped a bed frame too. "Now shove them together!" The four slid their upturned bed frames together just as the Foxes reached them. *Clink!* The couple wailed and clawed at the frames like animals trying to get in at meat.

"Push them back!" Poppy cried out from the spot where the two beds met, clasping the joint. But the Foxes were stronger than their wasted bodies made them appear.

Mr. Fox shoved hard, and the juncture of the two bed frames gave. Poppy and Marcus were pushed behind the frame on the right, separated from Dash and Azumi, who were struggling to hold the other one in place. Mr. Fox continued to force Poppy and Marcus backward toward the window. Across the room, Mrs. Fox grabbed at Dash and Azumi.

"There's a door right by you!" Poppy yelled to them. "Go!"

Marcus felt the doorknob pressing into his back. He swung the door open as Mr. Fox hoisted himself up and began to

24

climb the bed frame. Marcus grabbed Poppy's bag and hauled her through the dark doorway. As he pushed the door closed behind them, Poppy caught a glimpse of Dash and Azumi slipping through the opening in the opposite wall.

The house had split them up.

CHAPTER 5

DASH SLAMMED THE door shut and pulled the knob with all his weight. He could feel Mrs. Fox yanking it from the other side, twisting it back and forth. The knob started to slip through Dash's slick palms. "Azumi! A little help?" He felt her reach over his head. There was a click as Azumi flipped a bolt into place, and Dash loosened his grip on the knob.

"That woman's not getting in here," she said.

They were standing at the top of a set of spiral stairs. Black iron slats swirled into the shadows below, while a cracked skylight overhead barely illuminated the slim space.

"Ghosts." Dash shivered. His brother's face popped into his head, a perfect mirror of his own. "They said they were looking for Cyrus Caldwell."

"Yeah, they had 'an appointment.' Probably back when the orphanage was still open." Azumi shuddered. "I don't think they ever managed to leave."

"This is such a mess!" Dash cried out, covering his face with splayed fingers. "I should never have let Dylan out of my sight." His voice rebounded into the stairwell. *Out of my sight . . . my sight . . .* It sounded as if his brother were mimicking him. "And now we're all separated! It's like the house is doing this on purpose—trying to isolate us."

"We're not *all* separated." Azumi smiled wanly. "You have me! There's hope yet."

Dash tried to smile back, but he couldn't force his mouth into the right shape. "Thanks," he said. "I need to remember that." He took a deep breath, trying to calm down and think. "So. How do we get back to Marcus and Poppy?" he asked.

"Right now, we only seem to have one option," said Azumi. She nodded at the twisting staircase.

The Trickster hides in the darkness.

He makes his eyes wide, so the audience will see his performance from inside the sad clown mask that Del Larkspur gave to him.

Dash and that girl are coming down the spiral stairs. Their footsteps on the metal make a *bing-bing-bing* sound.

He knows the camera is out there somewhere, focused on his face, his mask. Everyone is waiting for Dash and the girl to reach the steps over his head. This will be the Trickster's time to shine, to make an impression on the director and the producer and the other members of the cast.

According to Del, Dash has no clue what is about to hit him.

The Trickster forces a snicker down his throat. Del was so right to put him and Dash in separate roles. He'd never imagined that playing an "evil" character would be so much fun.

The Trickster wonders if Dash is having fun too.

Bing-bing-bing.

The dark is closing in. The Trickster needs air. He reaches for the clown mask. His fingertips go prickly as he yanks it away, the plastic tugging at his skin as if the inside of the mask were coated in a thin layer of glue.

Strange.

Tremendous pain creeps across his hand. His mind flickers with disconcerting yet familiar images: his body atop a metal slab in a morgue, his family standing over an open grave, his brother's bed in the psychiatric ward . . . These aren't *memories*, are they? The Trickster drops the mask. It clatters to the floor, and the pain, the visions, everything evaporates.

A voice speaks in his head: *We only get one shot. Do not ruin this. You don't want to disappoint Del.*

Bing-bing-bing.

The footsteps are ringing louder now. Only one or two more turns around the spiral and then—

He bends down for the mask and then slips it back on. It feels more natural now, less tight. *Everything is fine.* He sighs.

"Do you hear that?" Dash's voice echoes from above.

The Trickster freezes, not wanting that inner voice to yell at him again, not wanting to feel that dripping pain, not wanting that flood of memories to—

"I don't hear anything," answers the girl. "What was it?"

"Breathing?"

He covers his painted, plastic frown with his hands. He's going to laugh and ruin everything!

"Come on, we shouldn't waste time," says the girl. "There's got to be a way for us to catch up to Poppy and Marcus."

Bing-bing-bing.

He feels his body buzz with excitement. The spiral staircase reverberates with their steps. The two are just overhead.

Any second . . . any second . . . any second now the Trickster will reach out from under the staircase and . . . and . . . and *snatch*—

Dash couldn't move his foot.

Something grabbed his ankle and twisted it. His body tumbled forward. Dash screamed, swinging his arms, reaching for the curved railing, but his forearms hit the edge of the iron steps below and the world flipped. His legs catapulted over his head, and he landed on his back on a flat cold surface.

His heartbeat echoed loudly in his ears, agony like an alarm clock, crying *wake up, wake up, wake up!*

Azumi rushed down the rest of the steps and crouched beside him, and Dash heard soft laughter echo out from underneath the stairs. He craned his neck to catch a glimpse of whoever was hiding there, but the sound stopped abruptly.

Had the laughter sounded familiar? It couldn't be. Could it?

Dylan! Dash struggled to call out, but his tongue refused to cooperate.

"Dash? Dash! Answer me!" Azumi was staring down at him. "Can you move?" Dash wiggled his fingers. Relief. He nodded and Azumi let out a breath. "What happened?"

"Someone . . ."

Azumi shook her head, confused. "Someone . . . what?"

Tripped me, Dash finished in his mind. "I-I lost my footing," he said aloud, closing his eyes, refusing to look again toward the darkness under the stairs.

CHAPTER 6

MARCUS AND POPPY were in a hallway drenched in late afternoon light. As the sun began to settle behind the distant line of trees over the grassy meadow, a saw blade of shadow crept up from the floor onto the wall across from old lead-paned windows.

Marcus turned away from the view, glancing back at Poppy. She was still kneeling, grasping the shuddering door-knob. "Poppy, we bolted the door," he said. "I don't think he can reach us anymore."

Worry filled Poppy's eyes. "What if he can *unbolt* the door?"

Marcus grimaced. He hadn't considered that. "How about you let go of the knob and see?" he said. "If the door starts to move, we can hold it shut until Mr. Fox tires himself out."

"Do ghosts *get* tired?" Poppy asked.

Marcus shook his head, trying to hold in his frustration. "The longer we stay here, the harder it'll be to find the others."

Poppy considered for a second. "Well, you're right about that."

"Gee, thanks," said Marcus, his throat tightening.

She slowly took her fingers away from the knob, her eyes glued to the bolt. It held. Poppy waited several more seconds before she finally leaned back. "That was . . . I can't believe . . ." She sighed and stood up. "Now how do we find Azumi and Dash? That was so stupid—I should've named a place for us all to meet!"

"Maybe this is better," said Marcus. "If you'd told them somewhere specific, like the game room or something, Cyrus might have made it impossible for us to reach it. You know? Like, he would've put up some sort of roadblock."

Poppy sighed. "So what do we do?"

"You're asking *me*?"

"Of course!"

"We walk," he said, trying to sound self-assured, surprised that she wanted his opinion. "Remember how my piano music led you and Dash downstairs to the ballroom when you were lost?"

Poppy blinked, unimpressed. "Yeah?"

"Same thing here. We'll call to them, and they'll probably be calling for us too. We'll find one another."

"That works," said Poppy, nodding to herself. Her eyes seemed glassy, as if she were already tired of him. "Just keep an eye out for the Foxes or anyone else you don't recognize."

They headed down the bright hallway, away from the dormitory. "*Dash! Azumi! Dylan!*" they called.

Behind them, Mr. Fox's phantom fists pounded at the door. On their left, several doorways opened into darkened rooms that they instinctively veered away from.

A warm breeze wafted toward them from farther down the passage. It was followed by a stench so horrible that both Marcus and Poppy had to stop and cover their noses.

"What is that?" Marcus asked.

Poppy shook her head, swallowing down her nausea. "Once, back in the city, there was a dead rat in the alley outside the bedroom window." She pointed in the direction of the breeze. "*This* is worse."

"I think I'm going to throw up," said Marcus.

"Breathe through your mouth." Poppy nodded them forward again. "Where do you think it's coming from?"

"An open grave? A sewer? Someone with *really* bad breath?"

As they walked, the breeze grew into a wind. Fierce gusts ruffled their clothes. And the stench only got worse.

A few feet ahead of them, there was a turn—a new hallway that snaked back into the depths of the house. A few dim sconces illuminated the familiar blue Gothic wallpaper. Marcus wondered if the heartbeat sound was still thumping through its dark vines—like the musical rhythms that used to dance through his mind. He hated how quiet everything was without it. "Dash! Azumi! Dylan!" he called out.

A gust of wind stopped Marcus in his tracks. "I can't stand this smell. We have to turn back," he said.

"Wait," said Poppy, standing at the junction. "I have an idea."

"I'm not going to like this idea, am I?"

"Rules of the real world don't seem to exist at Larkspur, right?"

"If you say so."

"I mean, everything we've experienced so far has sort of pushed us in certain directions," said Poppy. "Something didn't want me looking through the files in that office when we first got here, so a fire started. We found the door with the nails in it, and before we could even figure out what that was all about, a kid in a mask showed up and attacked. The Specials chase us

35

unless we get close enough to grab for their masks." Poppy frowned. "If the house and the things inside it are puzzles that Cyrus built, then maybe his solutions are in the places that are the hardest to reach."

"So you think *Cyrus* wants to keep us from going down that hallway," said Marcus. "The one where the wind is coming from."

"There's got to be something down there that he doesn't want us to see. Maybe even a way out."

"But if he can move the walls around, why wouldn't he just block off the hallway? Maybe he's playing some sort of reverse psychology. Like: *Don't go in there!*" Marcus cupped his mouth and whispered, "*But actually . . . do!*"

Poppy glared at him. "I don't know, Marcus."

"And what if it *is* a way out? Do we just leave the others?"

"I'd hate for that to be the case," said Poppy, stepping back into the breeze. "We'll figure it out later." The breeze lifted her hair from her scalp, pushing it off her forehead. For a second, Marcus was struck by how much she looked like the girl from the portrait they'd seen just before Dylan ran away. Consolida Caldwell—Poppy's *girl in the mirror.* The ghostly friend who had stood beside Poppy her whole life.

Marcus tried to smother a pang of jealousy. He'd had a

secret friend his whole life too, a musician who sent him bursts of notes, pieces of song that danced through his head and out his fingers. Everyone had called Marcus a prodigy, but he only cared about the music that wrapped around him day and night. It wasn't until he arrived at Larkspur House that Marcus discovered who the Musician really was: his uncle Shane, who had gone missing as a boy. Who was presumed dead. The songs were a protection for Marcus, but the house had silenced them. Now the quiet sounded so big Marcus was sure it would swallow him whole.

"Whatever," Marcus said, pushing down a sense of irritation that Poppy was probably right *again*. He pinched his nostrils tightly and then followed her into the foul wind.

CHAPTER 7

"OUCH, OUCH, OUCH!" Dash stiffened as he tried to stand at the bottom of the spiral staircase, leaning on Azumi's shoulder.

"It hurts that bad?"

Dash glared at her. "I'm not making it up!"

"You've just got to try harder," said Azumi, as if it were possible to simply ignore the pain that was shooting up his left leg.

His irritation made him take another step. "I guess I'll just hop around Larkspur from now on. This'll be fun." Dash groaned, loud and long, as if that would relieve the ache in his twisted ankle.

"Come on," said Azumi. "Let's find a better place to clean you up."

Dash glanced back toward the staircase. "Can you check under there before we go?"

Azumi's face paled. "Why?"

"Might as well search all corners. Right?"

She looked at him skeptically, then propped him against the doorjamb and stepped back toward the spiral steps. "Are you sure you didn't see something—"

"No!"

"You don't have to bite my head off, Dash."

At the top of the stairwell, the banging sound started again—Mrs. Fox at the dormitory door.

"I'm sorry," he said, shifting his weight uncomfortably. "Ever since I found out Dylan was . . . Let's just say my brain feels like my worst enemy."

Azumi stared at him for a moment. She walked into the darkness underneath the steps. Dash flinched, imagining a pair of hands reaching out from the shadows and closing around Azumi's throat.

"Dust bunnies," Azumi said, emerging from the gloom.

"Right," said Dash, still feeling tension in his rib cage. "That's good. Thank you."

They walked around a corner and slowly continued down another hall. Azumi was the one calling out to Dylan now.

This isn't real, Dash thought. *This is all a dream. Dylan is still alive. I must be asleep somewhere, in some other version of the world.*

Limping, Dash gritted his teeth to hold his hurt inside.

There's nothing like hurt to help you understand that you're wide awake.

"Dylan!" Dash shouted.

"Look, a bench!" Azumi pointed through an open doorway into a hall filled with amber light spilling in through glass walls. The bench was an intricate iron love seat, surrounded by lush plants that grew tall from the ground around it. A greenhouse. "C'mon. You can rest there."

They entered the glass hall. Dash groaned as he sat, and Azumi stepped away. "Where are you going?" he asked.

"I'll keep looking around. If I can find the others, I'll bring everyone back here."

"No way." Dash shook his head and tried to stand, only to sway from the pain.

"It'll be faster if I go by myself." Azumi leaned down so that their eyes were at the same level. "Don't worry. No one is leaving this house without you. I promise." Then quickly, before Dash could reach out for her, she turned and went for the door.

"Hold up!" he said, but she swung it shut. *Click!* "At least keep the door open!" Smiling through the window, Azumi gave a little salute and then ran off. "Azumi!" But she hadn't heard him.

Dash struggled to stand, then limped to the door. The handle wouldn't budge. He wiped his sweat-slicked palm on his shorts and tried again, but the door was stuck, or locked.

"*No*," he whispered.

He turned back slowly to take in his surroundings again. Through the glass overhead, whispery cirrus clouds brushed against the highest point of the blue sky. The sun had dipped below the tree line. His ankle throbbed and his skinned forearms stung as if with a bad rug burn. He was alone again. Trapped.

Dash pushed aside a few large leaves and then brought his face to the window. The grass out in the meadow glistened like wind-tickled waves. Escape seemed *so close*.

Could he trust that Azumi would make it back to let him out of here?

A white shape flickered across the meadow, tumbling end over end, as the wind picked it up and carried it straight toward him.

Slap!

Dash flinched as the paper smacked flat against the glass right in front of him. It was a sheet of newspaper. The headline near the top caught his attention, and he tilted his head to read: *Young Actor Still Missing*. And just below that was a photograph of him and Dylan standing together in front of the old studio lot. His heart pounded as he skimmed the article. *Escaped from an asylum . . . Twin killed . . . A national manhunt . . .* But the final bit made him feel like a ball of ice had lodged in his stomach. *The suspect should be treated with caution . . . Dash Wright may be dangerous . . .*

Another gust of wind snatched the paper up and away.

Dash fell back against the iron bench. He fought for breath as his throat constricted. *No*, he thought, *it's a trick. Like something Dylan would have done.* Dash forced himself to laugh and then called out, "You can't fool me anymore!" He wasn't even sure who he was talking to. Panic squeezed sweat from his pores.

Lowering himself, careful to avoid pressure on his ankle, he dug his fingers underneath the closest stone he saw and tugged it up, leaving a dark gash in the dirt. Leaning against the glass wall for support, he stood and swung the stone as hard as he could.

WHAP!

The stone bounced off the glass and fell to his feet.

Dashhh . . .

Was someone calling to him? He could have sworn a voice had whispered out to him, but now the room was eerily quiet.

He reached for the stone again and threw it with all his strength at the door. *Bam!* It landed askew beside the bench.

Dashhh!

The voice was harsher this time, more desperate.

"Dylan?" he whispered. He looked at the towering plants that tunneled into the distance. Were the trees taller now? Were the shadows darker? The inside of the greenhouse was actually beginning to look like a real forest. Dash swallowed. Was his brain breaking again? He pressed his arms against his rib cage, trying to make himself smaller, invisible.

There was a creaking sound behind him, like the pull of the ropes that held his parents' boat to the docks in Marina del Rey. He turned and grabbed the back of the iron bench. "Is someone there?"

Kreee. Kreee. Kreee.

"Dylan? Are you playing with me?" He thought of the

shadow under the spiral staircase. "It's okay if you are. I deserve it. I just want to . . . to *know*."

One of the large leaves rustled.

"This isn't funny!" Dash skirted the side of the bench and stepped across the stone path. But as he pushed the foliage aside, he realized his mistake.

A corpse swayed in a small thicket of trees—a space that couldn't have been there a moment prior. The bright pink noose around its neck was looped on a branch overhead. The body was a man of middle age, the front of his collared shirt smeared with gore. The dark hair on his grayish-green scalp was sparse. And the face . . . The face . . . Where there *should* have been a face was a mess of stringy black pulp. What was left of his skin had stretched, as if his jaw had long ago detached and pulled his features down with it. His eye sockets were wide pools of darkness, his nose was just an elongated oval hole, and his mouth was frozen in a silent shriek.

The noose swung slightly again. *Kree-eee-eee.*

Dash stumbled backward, a scream trapped in his throat. *This isn't real*, he told himself, as if he could blink and the corpse would simply disappear.

Instead, the rotting body shivered and jerked.

To Dash's horror, it raised an arm and clawed at the nylon

46

rope at its neck. The cord pulled tight and then snapped, and the corpse dropped to the dirt. It craned its head toward Dash, as if its empty eyes could see him. *Mmmmmm*. A rattling came from inside its shredded throat.

A hand fell on Dash's shoulder from behind him.

He yelped and swiveled out from under it, turning to find a familiar face only a few inches away. "Azumi!"

"Dash!" she hissed. "Be quiet!" Fear had turned her dark eyes huge. She was covered in dirt and grime, as if she'd just crawled through a ditch to get back to him. She grabbed his wrist and pulled him away.

But bony fingers clamped onto the back of Dash's neck, nails pressing sharply into his skin. He couldn't help himself—his shriek rattled his eardrums.

CHAPTER 8

BY THE TIME Poppy and Marcus reached the wide door at the end of the hallway, the wind was raging, pushing hard against them, growing hot and even more pungent. It was rot and bile and waste and death, and it was making their eyes water and their stomachs churn. Neither of them could tell where it was coming from.

"In here?" Marcus choked out, reaching for the knob. Squinting, Poppy nodded. The door swung inward, and as soon as they stepped over the threshold, there wasn't even a memory of a breeze. Poppy inhaled a deep, full breath of clean air, and Marcus did the same.

They were inside a large rotunda. The curving stone wall reminded her of the castle turrets she'd read about in *The*

Chronicles of Prydain and *The Sword in the Stone*. Outside four tall windows, Poppy could see the meadows and woods surrounding Larkspur. A thin staircase rose up against a far wall to a balcony.

"I don't see an exit here," said Marcus, his voice almost accusing. "And where was that wind coming from?"

But several tables around the room had caught Poppy's attention. Pieces of paper were strewn across one of them. Poppy could see drawings of large black dogs, lips pulled back to show sharp teeth. There was another illustration of what looked like an old-fashioned fair, with a carousel and a Ferris wheel and streamers and red balloons floating through the sky. At the very edge of the table was a crayon drawing of six figures—five that looked like children dressed in the familiar gray orphanage uniforms, and to their right, a taller figure in a black suit. Each of them had a name over their heads: *Gage, Sybil, Eliza, James, Orion*. The tallest figure was labeled *Cyrus*, and *1935* was written in the corner.

Poppy was overcome with a dizzying sense of nausea and disgust. Were the kids on this page more orphans that Cyrus had tormented, just like the Specials? Just like her? Feeling as though she'd discovered an important clue, she grabbed the drawing and held it to her chest, careful to not crumple it.

The next table over was messier—torn strips of paper were lying in piles and a metal bucket sitting on one end was crusted with white goo. "Papier-mâché," Poppy heard herself whisper.

In the center of the room were five desks covered in papers and a layer of dust. A plastic cat mask stared at them from one of the desks, and Poppy shuddered. A wooden chalkboard stood at the front of the room, dusty text written on it with bright white chalk.

The words *Hope* and *Fear* were written across the slate, each followed by a quotation.

"What's this all about?" Marcus asked, coming over to stand beside Poppy.

"Looks like a lesson. I guess this is a classroom?"

The door clicked shut behind them. They both turned, but no one was there. Poppy raced across the space and grabbed the knob.

"Don't open it!" said Marcus.

But she cracked the door a few inches and peered out into the hallway, bracing herself. No awful stench. No mysterious wind. "Just making sure it wasn't locked. It must've swung shut on its own."

"That wasn't smart," Marcus said, his voice clipped. "How

Hope

"Hope is the dream of
a waking man." - Aristotle

Fear

"Where no hope is left,
is left no fear." - John Milton

many other freaky things need to happen here before you stop and think first?"

"I *did* think about it first," Poppy shot back. "It just doesn't take me as long as you."

An uncomfortable quiet settled on them. Marcus's watery gaze made him look like he wanted to cry . . . or maybe scream at her. Poppy felt herself about to apologize when she saw that the blackboard behind him was now clear. She gasped.

Marcus leapt toward her, as if she could protect him. "What? What is it? Is someone there?"

Poppy shook her head and pointed. "Oh!" he said, noticing the board. "Well, *I* didn't touch it. I swear." The chalk had been smeared hastily. The only words still visible were *Hope* and *Fear.*

"I didn't say you did." Poppy approached the desks again, tentatively now. Marcus stayed close. "Is someone here?" she asked. "Connie? Is that you?" Then she tried, "*Matilda?*"

Marcus looked at her incredulously. "That's the name of one of the Specials, right? The girl in the cat mask? The one who spoke to us back in the music room—"

Poppy shushed him. A sound was coming from the other

side of the board, a slow scratching. "Listen," she whispered. "Someone *is* here."

Poppy stepped toward the chalkboard; the scratching stopped. She grasped the wood base and pulled it toward her. The chalkboard swiveled and then flipped upside down.

There was a new message written for them. Poppy read it aloud, her skin prickling. *"Not the Specials."* Looking up and around, as if someone were listening, she tried to keep her voice from shaking. "Are you going to hurt us?"

The sound came from behind the board again.

Scratch, scratch, scratch.

When it ended, Poppy cautiously reached out and flipped the chalkboard over.

Another message had appeared.

We are the first orphans.

"The first orphans?" said Marcus. "You mean . . ." He turned wide eyes at Poppy. "There were others?"

Poppy glanced at the page she'd taken from the art table. "Gage, Sybil, Eliza, James, and Orion," she read quietly. Marcus leaned toward her, examining the drawing from over her shoulder. "Are you . . . *good*?" Poppy asked.

"Like they'd tell us if they weren't!" Marcus whispered.

The scratching started up again. Then, to their surprise, the board turned on its own, revealing more words.

Not safe here.

It wasn't the answer Poppy had wanted, but it was better than reading *NO*. "Who's not safe here?" she called out.

"We're trying to find an exit," said Marcus. "Can you help?"

The board flipped. Instead of words, a chalk drawing appeared. A brooding young man. Crosshatching continued to add depth so that, for a moment, the man almost seemed to loom out of the flat surface. His face was long, with a sharp chin and a prominent brow. His cheeks were sunken and his lips were pressed together tightly so that they formed a severe line just below his long nose. A wild bush of hair sprung out from his head, as if he'd forgotten to brush it.

"Who's that?" Marcus asked. "He looks like a creep."

The man's eyes flicked toward them, as if daring Marcus to repeat himself. Poppy grabbed Marcus's wrist.

Chalk lines slowly appeared, scrawled across the man's forehead. *Cyrus Caldwell.*

More writing: *Your cousin, Poppy.*

"*No*," Poppy whispered, her voice hoarse. "I don't want . . ."

Marcus groaned and yanked himself away from her. Poppy

noticed little pink indentations on his skin, and she realized she'd dug her fingernails into his arm.

The light in the room shifted, turning paler and bright, as if it were early morning instead of late afternoon. The drawing of the man on the chalkboard seemed to glide forward, his skin and hair and clothes filling with color, and then he was there, in the room with them, standing before the row of desks that were filled with five children. Were these the first orphans?

"Poppy, what's going on?" Marcus whimpered.

Poppy forced herself to look at the young man's face. "I think it's just a vision, like how your uncle Shane appeared in the music room to help you. The orphans need us to *see* something."

"But what if the orphans aren't doing this?" asked Marcus. "What if it's someone much worse?"

CHAPTER 9

THE VISION CAME to life all around them, and brief scenes moved past Poppy and Marcus like images in a flip-book.

Gage could play the piano as well as any adult. Sybil was obsessed with books and reading. Eliza had a tendency to sleepwalk, but when she woke, she was able to recall vivid dreams about her missing sister, which Cyrus cataloged faithfully in his notebooks. James had never developed the ability to speak, but he shone with kindness and devotion to the others. In contrast, Orion was never quiet, full of energy and contagious enthusiasm that won him admirers during group trips into the nearby town of Greencliffe.

"The orphans," Poppy whispered, dread crawling up her

legs. "They're just like what we've learned about the Specials. Just like our group. It's like Cyrus has been seeking out the same types of kids over and over."

"I have a bad feeling about this," Marcus responded. "And I'm really cold."

Poppy realized that she too was freezing. The sensation had crept up on her so slowly that she hadn't noticed it. She struggled to pull air into her lungs, but she could get only a worryingly small gulp.

"I have a surprise for you," Cyrus proclaimed, standing at the front of the classroom. "A boat ride down the river to West Point!" His smile was odd, a little too tight. "How does that sound?"

Poppy's legs and hands were numb and prickly, and her hair clung to her skull as if it were wet. Marcus's face was pale.

They watched as the group piled onto the deck of the white, two-story vessel that Cyrus had chartered for them.

"Isn't this wonderful?" asked Cyrus, as the captain pulled the boat away from the dock. It was as if he couldn't see the children huddled together on the bench near the bow, cowering as the boat moved farther from shore. "So relaxing," he insisted, his voice like molasses as he pointed out landmarks along their way.

As they reached the middle of the wide river, there was a boom and a shudder as the engine burst, blowing a hole in the bottom of the boat. The orphans cried out and Poppy shrieked silently along with them.

Water rushed in from below, meeting the heat of the boiler, and steam hissed up into the air, mixing with smoke.

But one by one, the children's cries went quiet.

One by one they disappeared beneath the dark water.

Alone, his face blank, Cyrus calmly swam away from them toward the nearest shore. Poppy could feel the water close over her own head, forcing bubbles from her lungs. She kicked upward as hard as she could, frantic for air and the surface.

A hand clamped around her ankle and she felt herself being tugged beneath the surface. Air exploded from her mouth as she screamed. Looking down, she saw one of the orphan girls clutching at her, dragging her farther into the depths. She kicked at the girl's hand and strained toward the glistening ceiling of water over her head. But more fingers wrapped around her limbs. A boy and another girl had taken hold of her. Their hair swirled around their shadowed faces. Poppy squirmed, frantic, and saw Marcus a few yards away, held tightly by the other two children. His eyes were closed and his body thrashed.

They're killing us!

The five children screamed underwater. Their voices were muffled and distorted by the water pressing down on them, but Poppy could hear them anyway. *No! No! Help! Please!*

Poppy caught the eyes of the girl clinging to her leg. They glimmered with horror and fear. And Poppy knew: The orphans weren't trying to hurt them, at least not on purpose. The orphans were dying, *again*, and in their panic, they were pulling Marcus and her down with them.

Poppy's lungs were begging for air, but if she inhaled, she feared it would be a huge gulp of water and murk. She tried to think at the orphans, pleading for them to release her and Marcus. *We can only help you if we're free!*

But none of the drowning children would let go. Poppy could feel their minds whirling, out of control with fright. They only tightened their grip as they sank like anchors. The water grew darker, the bright surface overhead fading quickly, like a memory of a dream.

CHAPTER 10

THE CORPSE'S FINGERS dug deeper into Dash's neck, sending shock waves of pain down his spine. He could almost feel the corpse leaning toward him from behind, its sagging mouth aimed at the base of his skull.

Then, with a crash, the squeezing sensation was gone. Dash was free.

He spun to see the corpse flailing on the ground, the pink cord swinging wildly over its head. Beside it stood a girl, her fists clenched—not Azumi, but someone he didn't recognize. Her hair was a faded blue, as straight as straw, and bobbed just below her ears. She kicked at the thing as it tried to sit up again, knocking it flat.

"Go!" the girl yelled. "Go now!"

Azumi clutched his arm and tugged him back to the stone path. The other girl burst through the low branches and leapt ahead of them.

Following as quickly as he could, Dash hobbled along the path toward the shadowy tunnel of green. His right foot was sturdy, but his left was in agony.

From behind him came the sound of moaning as the corpse crashed out from the trees. He thought of its withered limbs, its pointed finger bones, and how deceptively strong it had been, and Dash hopped even faster.

The light grew dim as they pressed into denser foliage. The glass walls and ceiling disappeared entirely. Bright green moss coated thick tree trunks that rose up from the ground. In the back of his mind, Dash wondered how all of these plants, all of this *earth*, could fit inside even the largest of mansions.

Around a sharp turn, the girls swiveled off the path, dropping down into dense undergrowth. Azumi reached out and grabbed Dash's shirt, pulling him with them. He landed in the rocky soil next to her. A blanket of leaves overhead kept the three of them hidden. The other girl was crouched beside Azumi, muscles tensed, as if ready to spring up and attack again.

Dash groaned in pain, and Azumi shushed him

vehemently. Her deep brown eyes were pleading: *QUIET*. And despite his racing heart, he forced himself to be still.

Beyond the bushes, out on the path, footsteps whispered inches from his head. He clenched his eyes shut, wishing desperately that he could shake himself out of this nightmare.

The sound of the footsteps tapered away into unsettling quiet.

Curled up on the ground between Dash and the other girl, Azumi cocked her head, listening. "Is it gone?" she asked the new girl, who nodded confidently. Peering at Dash again, Azumi's eyes flashed with annoyance. "We were trying to warn you!" she whispered.

"That was you? Calling my name?"

"Both of us." Azumi nodded toward the other girl, whose blue hair seemed to glow in the dark, like moonlight reflecting off a moth. "This place is filled with . . . well, it sounds weird to say it out loud, but it's filled with dead people . . . who aren't quite . . . *dead*." Her eyes were wide and frightened. "They're ravenous."

Dash shuddered, still panting for air.

He couldn't take his eyes off the other girl. Azumi followed his gaze and a wide smile spread across her face, as if she were unable to contain a brief burst of joy. "Dash, this is my big sister. Moriko."

Dash flinched. "*Moriko?*" Azumi's *dead* sister? Dash tried to slow his breathing, but his heart wouldn't stop pounding.

Azumi bit at her lip. "Did Marcus mention . . . what happened to her?"

Dash nodded, looking at Moriko, who stared back at him, sizing him up. *Play along, Dash. Play along.* "I think he said . . . she was missing? That she got lost in a forest in Japan?"

"That's right," said Azumi. "We were visiting our auntie Wakame." Her voice was trembling, and she glanced over her shoulder at the green shadows behind them. "Moriko wanted to leave the path, and I wouldn't follow her. And then she was gone, and I've had nightmares about it ever since." Azumi paused, staring at her sister. "But here, in Larkspur, when I was just outside of the ballroom, I heard her calling to me. I followed her voice, and it led me into this greenhouse. This . . . *forest.*"

"I-I don't understand," said Dash. "That doesn't . . . You were just . . ." What was Azumi talking about? She was just with *him.* He glanced at Moriko again. "Are you like one of them . . . one of the Specials?"

Azumi cocked her head at him. "What are the Specials?"

she asked. She studied his swollen ankle and the dried blood on his forearms. "And what happened to you?"

Dash stared at her, aghast. "This is from when I fell down the stairs just now," he said carefully, eyes locked on her face.

"Oh my gosh! Are you all right?"

"You know I'm not!" Dash said. "You were right there when it happened. Right behind me! *Why are you acting like this?*"

"Like *what*?"

"Like . . . you hit your head or something. Like you lost your memory. *You've been with me the whole time!*"

Azumi's face drained of blood. "Dash, I haven't seen you in hours. Not since we first got here." Her words hit Dash like a shower of sparks. "Whoever was with you when you fell down some stairs . . . *that wasn't me.*"

CHAPTER 11

"POPPY! MARCUS!" A voice called out as the door slammed open. "Here you are! Thank goodness!"

Poppy felt her body jerk violently. The orphans' faces disappeared into shadow, their tight little fingers slipping from her skin. The swirling chaos of the river dropped away in one great splash, and she found herself back in the classroom, the solid wood of the floor underneath her feet. Weakened and breathless, she and Marcus both fell to the ground, choking and gasping for air.

"I need your help!" The voice resounded around the chamber. "Hey, are you two all right?"

Poppy forced her burning eyes open. Azumi was standing in the doorway, practically panting. Her black dress and denim jacket looked like a smudge against the light from the hallway behind her.

"Azumi! How'd you find us?"

"I heard shouting." Azumi cocked her head. "What happened to you guys?"

Marcus coughed and trembled, holding up his hands and watching them twitch. His eyes were red, and he wiped at them furiously. Poppy's chest heaved as she took in great gulps of air. They had been dying, and her whole body sagged with relief that they were safe now.

The chalkboard stood empty before them, and the desks looked dusty and untouched—exactly the same as they'd been before the orphans' vision had stolen Marcus and Poppy away.

Poppy smoothed out her shirt, trying to slow her racing thoughts. Sitting back on her heels, she gestured to the room. "We came here looking for a way out. But instead, we met more ghosts." She shivered. "They showed us what Cyrus did to them."

"They made us *feel* it," Marcus added quietly.

"Wait," said Poppy. "Where's Dash? Did he find Dylan?"

"That's the thing . . ." Azumi's skin was grayish, her eyes like deep pools. She looked like she was about to faint. Poppy dragged herself to her feet and rushed toward her. "He's hurt,"

Azumi said. "He tripped down some stairs and twisted his ankle. I had to leave him alone, but I'm not sure he's safe."

"Of course he's not safe!" said Marcus. "None of us are."

"Come with me." Azumi stepped out into the hallway, waving for them to follow. "He needs us. *Now.*"

"Okay, okay," said Marcus, wiping at his eyes. "This was a dead end anyway. Let's get out of here."

A scratching sound echoed from behind them. Marcus grabbed Poppy's elbow and spun her around so they could both see what had appeared on the board. It was a chalk drawing of a tall wooden door, a sunburst decoration on top of it.

Azumi's mouth dropped open. "What the . . . ?"

"We've seen this! When the Specials were chasing us!" said Marcus, his face lighting up. "The door was in the hall downstairs!"

Frantic writing appeared, scrawling across the drawing of the door.

HOPE

FEAR

HELP!!!!!

Poppy stepped back into the room. "But *how* can we help you?" A darker thought slithered into her head: *And after what you just did to us, why would we want to?*

"Maybe they want to help *us*," Marcus said to her. He called out to the room. "If we find *this* door, we'll find our way out? Is that what you're saying?" Something heavy dropped from one of the tables by the wall, clunking against the floor. Marcus ran to pick it up. He turned and grinned, holding up a hammer. "I think they just gave us an answer."

Poppy trembled, pressing her fingers to the sides of her skull. "I don't feel like we have any answers. We've been searching and searching, being as smart as we can. Why am I still so confused? The Specials want to hurt us. Or, they don't want to, but when they're wearing the masks they can't help themselves. The first orphans want to help us? How do we know who to trust? What are we supposed to do?"

Azumi sighed, frustrated. "We're supposed to go get Dash. Come on!"

Poppy glanced around the room again. The orphans' memories still clung to her skin, like the muck of the river. She had to leave this room now—she couldn't bear the lingering claustrophobia of the water.

But more important, she knew her friend was waiting for her.

CHAPTER 12

AZUMI'S WORDS ECHOED in Dash's head: *That wasn't me . . . That wasn't me . . . That wasn't me . . .*

The girl who'd closed the door, who'd trapped him with the hanging corpse, *had not been Azumi*. At least, that's what *this* Azumi had told him only moments ago, but his brain refused to believe it.

The air in the greenhouse was suddenly stifling. Dash dabbed sweat from his forehead.

"Are you okay?" asked the *new* Azumi. Or was she the *old* Azumi? "You look like you're going to be—"

Dash turned his head before throwing up on the ground.

"Sick," she finished, scrunching her nose and looking away.

He wiped his mouth and took a deep breath. "You mean you're not . . . Are you . . . ? Who are you, then?"

"I'm Azumi!" she said.

"I don't understand. If you're Azumi, then who's the girl who was with us ever since . . . I don't even *know* how long?"

"I have no clue."

"Why did you call for me just now, and not Dylan?"

"Your T-shirts are different colors," she said simply. "Where is Dylan? Where are *any* of the others?"

Dash's brain felt like it was short-circuiting. Could he tell this girl the truth? What *was* the truth, anyway? That his brother was dead? Would she think he was crazy? "It's a *really* long story. I don't know where to start. What about you, Moriko?" he forced himself to ask. "How did you get here? How did you find us?"

"I didn't just get *lost* in the forest in Japan," Moriko said, her eyes on her little sister. Dash felt his muscles tense. Again it felt crazy to think it, but he suspected that Moriko was a ghost too. "The forest is a special place, like Larkspur House is a special place. Strange. Beautiful. *Haunted*. These kinds of places are connected to one another, like hidden roads, or secret passages.

"Larkspur House can twist your thoughts and make you

71

believe things that aren't true. Or it can make you forget what was once important, so that you lose yourself entirely."

Dash felt his face flush as he found himself nodding along.

"Not all the ghosts are bad," said Moriko. "Some of the spirits here want to give you hope. Hope for the things that you've lost in your lives. Hope for learning the truth so you can move on. Hope for . . . *escape*."

Dash shook his head. "Nothing inside this place has given me hope. It's all made me feel insane."

"And I've just been scared the whole time," said Azumi.

"Oh, but of course you've had hope! Why else would you have followed the pink ribbon down the hallway, Azumi? Why else would you have called out my name? Hope is the fuel that keeps us . . . that keeps *you* . . . alive." Moriko sniffed. "But the funny thing about hope is that it always comes with a price. Worry. Fear. Anxiety. Once something is important enough to hope for, it attains a power over you. *Hope* and *fear* are tied together as tightly as the threads that . . . that join haunted places."

Frustration made Dash's vision spin. His forearms were beginning to throb again, and his ankle felt like someone was hitting it over and over with a heavy mallet. "So what do we *do*? How do we get out of here?"

Moriko met his gaze. "Right now, you need to bring the rest of your group back here. Then we'll all head deeper into the forest. It's the only way out of this place."

Dash rocked back on his heels, a feeling of warmth spreading in his torso. Then he remembered what should have been the most important part. *Dylan.* His throat went dry, making it hard to say the next part. "My brother's in trouble though."

"What kind of trouble?" asked Azumi.

"Trouble like Moriko's . . . *trouble*," he said, his voice tiny. Azumi stared at him in confusion. "He's a . . . Well . . . He's a ghost."

Azumi's jaw dropped and Moriko exhaled slowly, as if she'd suspected as much. "Go find him. Go find all of them," said Moriko, standing and peering out at the nearby path. "I'll teach Dylan all he needs to know."

"You can help him?" Dash asked, thinking of the spiral staircase and the laughter he'd heard coming from underneath it. "You can show him how to become . . . *okay* again?"

"I'd have to be a monster not to," said Moriko with a strange smile. She picked a long, sturdy stick off the ground, tested it, and passed it to Dash. "A crutch, for you," she said. She checked the path once more, then waved for Dash and Azumi to follow her back toward the door.

"It's locked," Dash called out.

But Moriko touched the knob, and it turned in her hand.

"I swear the door was locked," whispered Dash, limping up beside her, wincing with every step.

"Trust your instincts," Moriko told Azumi, "and you'll locate your friends. And when you do, bring them back here."

"Come with us!" Azumi threw her arms around Moriko's neck. "I just found you! I can't leave you again so soon!"

Moriko shook her head and rubbed Azumi's back. "I'd follow if I could. It'll only be for a few minutes. I promise."

Down the path, beyond the two girls, the foliage rustled. A groaning sound emerged from the greenish darkness. Azumi's eyes widened as Moriko grasped her shoulders and pushed her into Dash's arms.

CHAPTER 13

THE TRICKSTER KNOWS that everyone is waiting for him to make his next move.

There is a shifting in the darkness surrounding him. The production people are busy making sure that everything is set for the next shot. No one will speak to him. Del explained earlier that he needs to stay in character. According to Del, the stunt that he'd pulled while hiding beneath the spiral staircase was a big hit with the director. The only problem, in the Trickster's opinion, is that Dash's pratfall looked almost too spectacular.

The Trickster worries, as usual, that his twin will end up overshadowing him.

The aroma of fresh baked bread and food roasted in spices

wafts from the darkness. Someone is preparing dinner for the cast. The Trickster's mouth is watering. Until this moment, he hadn't realized how hungry he is. He turns to find the food-service table only several feet away. He listens for the sound of approaching footsteps—the cue that he should take his place. For now, the hallways are quiet.

He grabs a handful of chocolate candies, and then attempts to lift his clown mask to slip some into his mouth.

A voice screams in his head: *DON'T DO THAT!* Pain blooms behind his eyes. It swells until the Trickster drops the candies. Then it stops, gone, as if it had never happened.

I'll eat later, he tells himself, shaking. *After this next shot, I'll have a real break. I'll catch up with Dash and the others, and see if they have any fun stories about their time inside Larkspur House so far.*

But you can't, a deeper voice speaks again from within his head. *They'll need you in character. They'll always need you in character.*

The Trickster is getting tired of this voice that won't let him do anything. He opens his mouth to argue, but then his mind flashes back to the searing pain he feels whenever he moves the mask. He snaps his mouth closed.

Footsteps echo from down the hallway. *It's the cue*, he thinks. *They're finally coming.* He steps backward, hiding inside a ragged opening in the wall.

The Trickster holds a defiant snicker inside. He can't give away his position. This time when they take off down the hallway, he'll chase them. And he'll be screaming like crazy. The camera will zoom in for a close-up, and he'll be laughing and laughing and laughing. The director will love it.

The footsteps come closer, accompanied by voices now.

"Wait, you guys," says Marcus.

What's that in his hand? the Trickster wonders. "I think we've been here before."

"It's the door the orphans drew on the chalkboard!" Poppy says. "The one with the nails!"

Marcus suddenly turns toward where the Trickster is hidden. "We've made a giant circle. It's like what you said before, Poppy, about exploring the places that are hard to get to. This is probably the hardest door to open in the whole house!"

Azumi groans, grabbing Marcus's sleeve. "Dash is probably freaking out by now. Come on, we've got to get back to the greenhouse."

Dash is freaking out? Big surprise, thinks the Trickster.

Poppy stares at the door with the nails, nodding. "The last time we were here, something was scratching from the inside. Is it safe?"

Azumi throws her hands in the air. "I'll tell you one thing you won't find behind that door—Dash! He wasn't in good shape when I left him. And he's probably in worse shape now!"

Ooh, nice, thinks the Trickster, leaning forward. Quibbling in the ranks! It might just be the perfect time to—

Heavy hands fall on his shoulders, and he lets out the tiniest gasp before he can help himself. He tries to turn his head to see who it is, but the mask blocks his view. Thick fingers squeeze the muscles near his neck, almost too hard. His stomach squelches. Has he done something wrong? Is the director displeased?

"We have to figure out what's inside. It might be the way out! We'll go back for Dash as soon as we have a look," Poppy says, pressing her ear against the door. After several seconds, she adds, "It's quiet now. I don't hear anything at all."

"Great," says Marcus, lifting the claw side of his hammer toward the closest nail. He catches it, twists his wrist, and the nail drops to the floor.

The hands on the Trickster's shoulders pull him backward

into the passageway so quickly that he nearly trips. He is turned around, surrounded by shadow, the voices of Poppy, Marcus, and Azumi fading behind him.

It's okay, says the voice in his head. *The director doesn't want to disturb anyone.*

"Del?" he whispers. "Is that you?"

The producer must need the Trickster for something more important than nails in a door. As the guiding hands push him farther into the dark, he senses many eyes watching from the shadows.

"Where are we going?" he asks the man behind him.

But the only answer is a long, soft, *Shhhhh.*

CHAPTER 14

"DOES THIS HALLWAY look familiar to you?" Dash asked Azumi, holding up the light from his phone. "I feel like I've been past here before."

"I can't tell anymore," she said. "Everything is dark and makes me nervous. I just want to go back to the greenhouse."

Dash kept walking, his new crutch knocking rhythmically against the floor. "Moriko pushed us out of there for a reason. We have to find the others. Find my brother."

"Wait—what's that?" Azumi whispered at him. "Who's there?" she called out.

In the distance, a shadow seemed to move. A whitish face hovered in the darkness, its features unclear.

"Cyrus?" said Dash, his esophagus constricting as his skin went cold. "Is that you?"

Dash stepped closer. It couldn't be Dylan, could it? *No way,* he thought. Not unless Dylan was wearing makeup. Or maybe a mask. But why would—

Azumi sidled up beside Dash.

Dark laughter tumbled down the corridor, and the figure broke into a run. Dash and Azumi clung to each other, frozen, watching as the pale face became clearer. A deep frown. A bulbous nose. Arched black eyebrows. Was it another orphan? A new Special? The thing barreled toward them, arms outstretched, a clown with red lips in the center of its face like a wet splotch of blood. A muffled scream broke out from within the mask.

Dash and Azumi snapped out of their shock, turned, and ran. The crutch thumped hard on the floor as Dash hobbled as fast as he could on his hurt ankle. Terrified by whatever was behind them, they ran without thinking, pushing harder and harder to move forward. But the air felt thick, like glue, and Dash could hardly catch his breath.

The yowling behind them grew louder as the walls narrowed. The blue wallpaper with the Gothic pattern gleamed in the bouncing light of Dash's phone. The familiar thumping sound echoed out—*whump-whump, whump-whump*—as the paper's velvet overlay began to throb out a heartbeat upon the satin.

Dash watched in horror as the lines on the paper began to undulate. Then, with a sticky, sucking sound, the velvet and satin separated. Yards of dark vines swelled into the hallway, searching the space like tiny tentacles floating in deep ocean water.

"Don't let them touch you!" Dash yelled. Azumi whimpered and slowed. He grabbed her arm, but she jerked to a stop, letting out a screech as her head was yanked backward.

"*Yowwch!*"

Dash turned to see a cluster of the blue tendrils clutching the end of Azumi's long hair, cinching it like a ponytail.

"Let go of her!" he cried out. He pulled hard at Azumi's jacket. There was a hissing sound from where her hair met the velvet vines, and then suddenly, her hair broke, dark strands falling to the floor. Several more of the vines reached toward them. Dash grabbed Azumi's arms again, and this time when he pulled, she came with him.

From behind them, the boy in the clown mask screamed with laughter. Dash and Azumi dodged the vines that continued

to stretch toward them. Ahead, they made a turn. The walls in this new corridor were wood. No more wallpaper. No more vines. "This way!" yelled Dash, pivoting and towing Azumi along.

Daylight spilled in through a window, just bright enough to show three figures nearing the other end of the hallway.

"Poppy! Marcus! Dylan, is that you?!" Dash called, so relieved to have found them that he stumbled along even faster. But Azumi skidded to a halt when the figures turned, grabbing Dash's elbow to slow him too.

Three masked children stood looking at them, the plastic over their faces shiny and bright, as if freshly cleaned. The children wearing the cat and bear masks blocked the path forward. And the boy in the rabbit mask stood off to the left, just inside a gaping hole in the wood wall.

"Do you think you can take them?" whispered Azumi, panting.

"Are you crazy? No way. Not just the two of us." Dash turned, glancing around, bracing himself for another attack. The Specials stared blankly at him, as if trying to steal his focus. But then he noticed a tall door to his right, a wooden sunburst shape crowning its top. "I've been here before," he whispered to Azumi.

Thick iron nails were scattered all over the floor, bent and broken, as if someone had yanked them from the splintered door frame. And the door was open a crack.

The horrible clown rounded the corner, shrieking with laughter that died when he saw the Specials at the other end of the hall. They leapt forward, and Dash and Azumi shoved at the door with the sunburst. Dodging small swiping hands, the two slipped inside, slamming the door behind them.

CHAPTER 15

DASH AND AZUMI pressed their full weight against the door, holding it shut. Dash's whole body heaved with breath. He felt for the sturdy latch by the doorknob and turned it, listening to the heavy *click* of the lock falling into place. "You all right?" he asked Azumi, wheezing.

She nodded, her jaw slack as if she couldn't believe what had just happened. What was *still* happening. "Those were the Specials you told me about?"

Dash nodded. He waited, tensed, for the Specials to start pounding from the other side. They were probably waiting to catch them off guard. He tried again to slow his breathing.

A faint light seeped in through the tall, thin windows to

the huge wooden table in the center of the room. Between each window was a bookcase, some filled with faded leather-bound books, others with taxidermied animals with unnerving black glass stares. A large, dusty crystal chandelier loomed over the table. The stale air was musty, as if the door they'd come through had been shut for decades.

"Earlier today," Dash whispered, "we heard something scratching from in here."

"Well, *that's* creepy," said Azumi, hugging herself. "But it looks like whatever it was is gone now."

"The door was nailed shut. I wonder who opened it?" Dash listened for movement out in the hall, but it was as if the entire house had gone silent. Where had the Specials gone?

There was movement underneath the table in the center of the room—a soft shiver of fabric shifting, the weight of a body settling.

Dash and Azumi went still, staring at each other with wide eyes. Dash forced himself to reach for the switch on the wall. The chandelier glowed, casting little rainbows on the floor and ceiling and walls.

"Who's there?" Azumi called out, her voice wobbly.

One of the wooden chairs shuddered and then slid away from the table. Dash raised his crutch like a club.

Someone emerged from under the opposite side of the table and stood, a pink messenger bag on her shoulder.

"Poppy!" said Dash, flooded with relief.

"Oh thank goodness!" said Azumi. "We thought you might be—"

Someone else rose up beside Poppy, his red curls glistening in the light overhead. "And me," said Marcus. He gasped when he saw them. The skin around his eyes looked almost bruised with worry.

"What's wrong?" asked Dash, feeling silly as the words escaped his mouth. What's wrong? Only *everything*!

To his surprise there came the sound of someone else shifting underneath the table. Dash's heart clenched. Had Poppy and Marcus found Dylan? But when the next person stood, both he and Azumi yelped, stumbling backward away from the group.

"Who are *you*?" yelled Dash. The girl standing between Poppy and Marcus looked exactly like the girl who was cowering beside him. It was Azumi.

Both girls wore identical expressions of horror, as though they couldn't believe what they were seeing: a double of themselves.

"She's Azumi," said Marcus. His lips were white, as if he

was about to vomit. Nodding at the girl beside Dash, he asked, "Who's *that*?"

"*I'm* Azumi," said the girl beside Dash.

"What's going on here?" asked Marcus. "Dash, where did you find this . . . this thing?"

"I'm not a thing!" shouted the Azumi by Dash. The only difference between her and the other girl was the dirt on her clothes and the blunt hank of hair cut short by the vine. "I'm your *friend*, you jerk!"

"I found her where *she* left me." Dash nodded at the other Azumi. "Inside the freaky old greenhouse."

"I told you I was going to get help," the girl answered. "I swear, I was bringing everyone back to help you when they found this door. Right?"

Poppy nodded. "We thought it would be a good idea to open it."

"I don't care about that!" said the Azumi with the short hair, her voice rising. She held her hands out at the long-haired version of herself. "What are we going to do? There are two of me!"

"Azumi never said anything about having a twin," said Poppy, fake cheer in her voice, as if she was struggling to find the perfect answer to this weird problem.

"I don't have a twin!" yelled Azumi with the short hair. "I

only have one sister. Her name is Moriko and she's waiting for us back in the greenhouse. She's going to get us all out of here. And *that*"—she pointed at the girl standing between Poppy and Marcus—"is not her."

"How dare you?" said the Azumi with long hair, leaning forward and clutching the edge of the table. "How dare you even say my sister's name?! Moriko is dead. Whatever is left of her is lying in a forest in Japan, at the base of Mount Fuji. I haven't seen her in a year. Nobody has!" She finished with a disgusted sneer. "I don't know who you are, or what you are, but if Cyrus Caldwell put you up to this, he's even sicker than we've all imagined."

Dash could feel the Azumi beside him trembling. Then, all at once, she was across the room, scrambling onto the wide table. She jumped, tackling the other Azumi, her momentum tumbling them both back toward the bookshelves several feet away, a tangle of arms and legs and identical denim jackets.

"Stop it!" screamed Poppy as the girls hit each other, clawing clothes and hair and skin. Memories of Thursday's Hope flickered through her brain—the girls who fought like this every week, the girls who would attack her with words and sometimes fists. She leapt onto the two Azumis, jamming her hands between them, forcing them apart. "Help me!" she yelled to Marcus and Dash.

Shaking off their surprise, Marcus and Dash rushed in, grabbing the two Azumis and pulling them backward. The Azumis continued to kick at each other even after they were dragged apart.

Poppy slid one of the wooden chairs into the space between them. "Why are you doing this, Cyrus?!" she yelled. Her voice echoed off the ceiling, as if that's where the orphanage director was hiding, watching with silent glee at the sick mess he'd created.

"This is what he wants!" said Poppy. "Don't you see? Everything here is trying to divide us up. We have to stick together. You have to calm down. Now!"

Eventually, the girls grew still.

"That's a nice thought and all, Poppy," said Dash, his hands looped under one Azumi's arms, grasping the back of her neck, "but it doesn't change the fact that there are two of the *same person* here with us." He glanced over to where he had come in. "The last thing we need is for—" He stopped talking, his face a mask of horror. "*Where did the door go?*"

CHAPTER 16

EVERYONE WHIPPED THEIR heads around to look. The wall where the door had been was now solid, covered with dark floral wallpaper. Their exit was gone.

"What?!" Poppy cried out. "How?" She stood and then rushed over to the wall, sliding her palms around as if it would just appear again if she found exactly the right spot.

The door's gone! Marcus fought against the churning in his stomach. "There's our answer, Poppy," he said quietly. "In a house that changes shape, why would someone need to nail a door shut? To make us curious about what was behind it."

"Then the door *was* a trap?" asked the girl in Marcus's arms. She rubbed at her chin, where a bright-red bruise was starting to appear. She ducked her head and then slid away from him.

The other Azumi scooted back from Dash and crouched at the edge of the nearest bookcase.

"Obviously!" said Marcus. "Those 'orphans' we met tricked us. *Oh, yeah, go looking for that door with the nails. Here, take a hammer so you can get through! We're oh so helpful!*"

Poppy blinked and then turned slowly, taking in the room.

"What is it, Poppy?" asked Marcus. "What bright idea do you have now?"

"Nothing. Not yet. It's just . . ." Poppy glanced at the group, eyes wide. "I don't believe it. I don't think those orphans tricked us at all. What if there's something here in this room, a clue about Cyrus, that will help us get out?"

"Out of the room?" asked Dash.

Poppy shook her head. "Out of the house! Maybe there's a secret passage or a door. We just need to find it."

The light outside was growing dimmer, turning the room an even deeper shade of blue. Evening was coming quickly.

"I don't care what we do," said short-haired Azumi. "And I don't know what you're talking about. All I know is that I'm finding my sister again if it kills me."

"Do you think you can do that without trying to kill me first?" asked long-haired Azumi.

"You don't get a say," said Dash, glaring at her. "And you don't get to argue. Neither of you. Not anymore. Not until we figure out what's going on with the two of you."

"Just stay away from me," said long-haired Azumi, nodding at the other. She patted the bruise on her chin and winced. "Or I promise I'll make you sorry."

Marcus sighed and crossed his arms. Poppy hiked her messenger bag higher on her shoulder.

"Look, there's no door anymore. We can't go look for Moriko; we can't go find Dylan. So what *can* we do? We might as well start exploring," said Dash. "Poppy, what did you have in mind?"

Poppy cleared her throat. It felt weird to go back to trying to figure things out. She hadn't even gotten a chance to ask Dash how he was or if he'd found any traces of Dylan. He was limping, his ankle looked really swollen, and he had a thick stick he was using as a crutch. What had happened? "I was thinking that maybe the orphans we met in the classroom gave us hints about how to get out," she said.

"They wrote messages on a chalkboard," said Marcus. "Stuff about *Hope* and *Fear*. Very helpful."

Dash turned to the short-haired Azumi, who was still hunched by the wall at the corner of one bookcase. "Moriko mentioned something about hope and fear too. How they're tied together. Once something is important enough to hope for, it has power over you. Once you have hope, you start to fear. Something like that?"

The other Azumi, the one with long hair, spoke up. "If your orphans could write messages on the chalkboard, why wouldn't they just give us all the answers we need?"

"Maybe they didn't have time," said Poppy, trying to keep her voice positive. "Maybe it's more complicated than a simple, *go here, do this*."

"At least there's one good thing about that door disappearing," said Marcus.

"And what's that?" asked Poppy.

"None of the house's horrible residents can reach us now."

The Azumi standing beside Marcus touched her chin again. "Unless one of them is already in here with us," she said.

CHAPTER 17

THE TRICKSTER IS confused. He is standing in the hall at the spot where Dash and Azumi disappeared through a doorway. But now that doorway is gone.

The other kids stand far away from him, watching, their arms crossed.

Footsteps stomp toward the Trickster from deep within a dark hollow in the opposite wall. He cowers as the floor shakes, hugging himself tightly. The sounds stop suddenly and a tall figure shifts within the space, hidden in the shadows several feet away.

Del's voice calls out to him, "*Trickster!* What were you thinking?"

"I was trying to—"

But Del cuts him off. "Why did you chase them this way? They weren't supposed to leave that hallway back there! We needed the group to be separated, and now they're all stuck together, and this is *all . . . your . . . fault.*"

The Trickster glances at his cast mates. They stare back wordlessly, as if they're all too disgusted to say anything. His face feels like it's burning inside his clown mask. He almost tries to take it off again, but then he realizes that might get him in even more trouble. Bad memories from the television studio flood through his body—him getting scolded for playing his jokes, his parents taking away his video games as punishment, Dash rolling his eyes and refusing to talk to him. The Trickster's old defenses rise up. "Nobody told me what to do! You just grabbed me and then shoved me toward Dash and Azumi. They're the ones who didn't run the right way. Why aren't you yelling at them?"

"Have you read the script?" asks Del.

The Trickster feels a jolt. The script! When was the last time he saw it? Had he ever even glanced at it after Del first handed it to him? Shame pierces his skin like a hundred little snake bites. "Can't we just do it over? I'm ready. Isn't everyone else?"

"I should have listened to the rumors about you," Del

whispers. "You'll follow the others from now on. At least they know what they're doing." The masked kids step forward. The Trickster stumbles away, suddenly afraid of what they might do to him.

"So much for your *big role*. I should have given it to your brother," Del says.

"I can do better," says the Trickster, shaking with embarrassment and anger. Can Dash hear all of this from the other side of the wall? Is he hiding a grin? "I promise."

"Don't disappoint me again," says Del, his silhouette shrinking back into the dark chasm.

CHAPTER 18

POPPY PULLED SEVERAL of the leather-bound books from the shelves and laid them out on the table in the center of the room. Bad thoughts nagged at her, about the Specials, about the orphans, about Cyrus, about the fact that somehow she had ended up in charge even though she had no idea what she was doing. She felt dizzy with dread. The others were going through the shelves behind her. She noticed that Marcus and Dash were standing between the two Azumis, keeping them apart, as they flipped through the materials.

Poppy bit at her lip, trying to focus. Opening one book, she nearly gasped. A picture of a baby in a bassinet stared up at her. The eyes were unmistakable. This was Consolida Caldwell, her Girl in the mirrors, as a baby. She had chubby cheeks and tufts of hair sticking straight up from her round little head. More photos showed a family at the very beginning of the twentieth century, when Connie had been a toddler. She aged as Poppy turned the pages. One photograph showed Connie— looking just like she had whenever Poppy had seen her in the mirrors—clutching an infant. Below the image, a silver pen had spelled out: *Loving sister holds Cyrus for the first time.*

"Anyone find anything useful?" asked Dash.

"The sun's sinking quickly," said one of the Azumis.

"Are we going to be stuck in here all night?" asked Marcus.

Poppy was too engrossed to respond. A few pages later, she discovered another picture of Cyrus, age twelve, with cautious eyes and that puff of crazy hair. She thought of the orphans' vision, of the man Cyrus would grow into, and she wondered if she could see a hint of his future heartlessness in the way his mouth turned down at the edges.

"Whoa," said Dash. Poppy jolted to attention and saw that he was sitting right next to her, going through another of the albums. "This is horrible." He turned the book so Poppy could see it.

This one was filled with newspaper clippings. One head-line from a local paper in 1912 read: *Mother and Daughter Perish in Nursery Fire at Hudson Valley Mansion.*

Poppy's skin went cold. A lump rose in her throat. She leaned forward to read, blinking repeatedly as the print and the photography continued to blur and blur and blur.

Greencliffe, Jun. 1. An early morning fire in the upper floors of Larkspur House resulted in the deaths of two members of the Caldwell family today. Frederick Caldwell, master of the house, awoke to cries from servants Ada Small and Florence Bland, who alerted him to smoke on the third floor. Caldwell's wife, Eugenia, age 32, and his daughter, Consolida (Connie), age 12, were overcome while trying to rescue his son, two-year old Cyrus, from the nursery. Miss Small was able to carry the boy to safety, but mother and daughter died minutes before Greencliffe's fire brigade reached the estate. Mr. Caldwell, a well regarded landscape and portrait painter, was unable to give a statement. The boy is currently under observation at the new Peekskill Hospital south of Greencliffe.

This is the second tragic event to strike Larkspur House recently—

The rest of the article was torn away.

Marcus and the two Azumis were reading over Poppy's shoulder. She pushed her chair back from the table. "Maybe this is what the orphans wanted us to learn," she said, smoothing her hair. "The truth about what happened here."

"Why would it matter to them?" asked Marcus.

"I don't know," she whispered. But it mattered to her! She couldn't help wondering what Connie's final moments had been like. She studied Connie's calm features in the photograph. Had Connie known that her baby brother would survive? Could she have imagined that he'd grow up to become a monster? She flipped back to a page that contained Connie's photograph.

Where did you go, Connie? she thought. *I still need your help . . .*

Poppy's insides buzzed as Connie's eyes in the photograph slowly slid up—she was still here with Poppy! She was trying to help! Connie seemed to be staring fixedly up and over Poppy's shoulder as if wholly focused on something. Poppy wheeled around, taking in the slim windows, the books, the bookcases, the stuffed fox, rabbit, and bobcat in a line on top. What was she missing? Poppy stood and whispered to Connie, "Are these what you want me to see?"

Dash followed her. "Doesn't it kind of look like they're chasing one another?"

"But why would a rabbit be chasing a fox?" asked the short-haired Azumi.

"It wouldn't," said Poppy. "I mean, everyone knows that rabbits are terrified of predators. You can see it in this one's

eyes." She leaned closer to the rabbit. "*Fear* of getting caught. *Hope* that he'll get away. Is that too much of a stretch?" She lifted the rabbit by the circular wooden base, not wanting to touch the patchy fur but hoping to look at it more closely. Something clicked and she noticed a panel built into the top of the bookcase. The rabbit had been weighing it down. "Whoa! There's some sort of mechanism here."

"Like a booby trap?" asked one of the Azumis.

"Careful, Poppy," said Dash.

"I don't think it's like that," she answered, glancing back at the album on the table. Was Connie smiling? Poppy brushed away chills, hoping that the others didn't notice that she was trembling. "Hopes and fears. Predators and prey," she whispered as if to herself. "The house is a mystery. A puzzle. *A fox chased by a rabbit chased by a bobcat* doesn't make sense. Does it? But if we put the rabbit first—" She slid the fox back to where the rabbit had been sitting. Another click echoed in the room. "Then we see how hope and fear are supposed to work together. Bobcat chases fox. Fox chases rabbit. Rabbit runs!" She placed the stuffed rabbit onto the spot where the fox had been.

The room rattled, and everyone looked around, startled. Then, by a far wall, a panel in the ceiling opened like a jaw, and a small set of stairs slid down to the floor.

CHAPTER 19

"IT WORKED!" MARCUS cried out. "I can't believe that actually worked!"

"Why not?" asked Poppy, grinning wide.

Marcus pressed his lips together. His fingers itched for the bow of his cello and all of him yearned for just one measure of his uncle's music to pour into his brain and calm him down. The longer he went without hearing it, the more alone he felt.

Dash stared into the darkness. "Are we really going up there?"

"There's no other way out of this room," said one of the Azumis.

"But Dylan's not—"

"We don't know where Dylan is," said Poppy, taking his

shoulders gently and steering him toward the stairs. He jerked away from her grip, and Poppy flinched, hurt. "I'm only trying to help."

"Sorry," mumbled Dash. "It's just . . . I've been pushed around enough today."

Marcus hung back, watching as the short-haired Azumi trailed Poppy and Dash up the stairs. The other Azumi caught his arm, pulling him close.

To his surprise, she threw her arms around his neck and burst into tears. Her sobs shook him as the others disappeared up into the ceiling. "What's wrong?" he asked.

"What's *wrong*?" She pulled away, her lip quivering. "Other than that girl showing up and trying beat me into a pulp?"

"Oh." Marcus blushed. He'd never been good at relating to people. "Yeah, it's all pretty disturbing."

"I thought I was doing okay, that we were going to all make it out. But now this! I don't know what to do. Everyone is suddenly looking at me differently, like *I'm* the bad person." She wiped at her nose.

"Everyone is just confused. They want to protect themselves."

"*You* know who I am though. You'll help me, right, Marcus?"

"Yes, of course," he said quietly. But *did* he know? Could he be sure?

Azumi closed her eyes. "I'll help you too. Whatever it takes." She threw her arms around him again and squeezed. Marcus tensed, then relaxed. It was almost like his uncle's music was swirling through his mind once again.

A sound caught his attention. Gazing over Azumi's shoulder toward the far wall, Marcus saw the missing door suddenly reappear. His jaw dropped in shock and he stepped back. Azumi turned to look as the door creaked slowly open, a small, pale hand clutching at its edge.

The Specials were coming!

"Go!" Marcus whispered, pushing Azumi toward the staircase. His thoughts reeling, he leapt toward the bookshelf where the taxidermy animals were sitting, swung his arm, and knocked them off the shelf.

A howl filled the room, sending chills up Marcus's back.

The stairs began to retract up into the ceiling. Azumi was already near the top, eyes wide, clutching the railing as if to keep the stairs from leaving him behind. Marcus jumped and landed a foot on the bottom step. He could hear the Specials pattering swiftly across the floor behind him. Azumi took one hand off the railing and yanked Marcus farther up the stairs, just as a spring-loaded mechanism slammed the panel shut with a resounding *whack!*

On the next level, everyone turned to look at them. "The Specials are coming!" Marcus shouted. "They managed to open the door downstairs. I knocked over the animals, but we need to get out of here before they solve the puzzle."

Poppy took a deep breath as if gathering her courage. "I have another idea," she said. "What about trying to set them free? We know how to do it. We did it once before. It's got to be tied to getting out of here."

"We can't!" said Marcus. "Even if we could get their masks off, we still have to give them something they need. We don't even know what that might be!"

"We've got to get out of here," Dash agreed. "But there's no door in this room either." His breath was coming quickly again.

"Then we're trapped?" asked short-haired Azumi. "Again?"

The other Azumi was standing beside a small round table in the center of the room. She ran her fingers along the edges of three circles that were embossed into the darker wood. "Unless there's another puzzle that opens another way out," she said.

Poppy and Dash glanced toward some wooden cupboards

with glass-paned doors. Inside the cupboards were a great number of glass jars.

"It looks like there just might be," said Poppy.

A smashing sound echoed up through the floorboards, as if one of the bookshelves had toppled over.

"Someone do something!" yelled Dash.

Marcus fought the instinct to hide in a corner. The key to getting out of this room had to be right in front of them. *Maybe this time*, Marcus thought, *I'll figure it out myself.*

CHAPTER 20

AS THE OTHERS rummaged around the room, the long-haired Azumi waved discreetly to Marcus from her spot by the window.

She nodded at the tabletop. A row of test tubes held cloudy blue liquid, each one darker than the last. A couple of jars were stuffed with deep-purple dried flower petals. In the middle of the table, a notebook was lying open, pale light spilling on it through the window. "What's all this about?" Marcus asked. Azumi held her finger to her lips.

He leaned closer and read.

April 13, 1938

Aunt Emily's package of larkspur flowers arrived today. She sent both types. Out west, the flowers grow in the wild, but here in the east, they're impossible to find. The consolida is more delicate looking than the delphinium. Lovelier. I can understand why it was my father's favorite blossom and why he named my sister after it.

I've read that the delphinium is more poisonous.

My mother's recipe calls for—

Marcus looked up at the girl beside him. "This is Cyrus's notebook!" he whispered. "What was he doing with these plants?"

"Making poison?" She plucked two of the glass vials from the rack. "Maybe the poison was for the orphans! Could this guy get any creepier?" She shoved one of the vials into the pocket of her denim jacket and handed the other to Marcus.

"What are we going to do with it?" asked Marcus.

"It might come in handy later on. We could use it for . . . for protection."

"Protection? But we don't know what it does."

Azumi frowned. "That girl just attacked me, Marcus. We all need to watch out for her."

Marcus's brain stopped producing words. He wished again for the music that used to haunt him to return, if only for a moment. Marcus shook his head and grabbed the notebook from the table. "Poppy will want to take a look at this."

"You're right," said Azumi coldly, opening a desk drawer and sifting through it. "It might help her understand a little more about the Caldwell family. That seems to be important to her. As important as *survival* is for the rest of us."

A loose page slipped from the notebook. Marcus caught it before it fell to the floor. He glimpsed a bit of writing at its top. *Dear Mrs. Geller . . .*

Mrs. Geller, his *mother*? What was a letter to Marcus's mother doing in Cyrus's journal? Marcus scanned it quickly and realized that it was from his cello instructor at Oberlin. Certain words and phrases leapt out from the page: *Painful lessons . . . Average talent . . . not sure your son should continue with me . . .*

He felt nauseated. Oberlin didn't think Marcus was any good?

They had made him believe that he was an actual *prodigy*. Suddenly, Marcus couldn't remember if they'd ever said that word, or if he'd come up with that idea on his own. His hand shook as he thought of the Musician and of how he'd mimicked his music. He'd tricked people into believing that it was his own. Maybe he *didn't* have any real talent.

He was suddenly furious that his uncle Shane had deserted him. Why show up at all if he was just going to leave? It had been Cyrus, Marcus thought, fuming. *Cyrus* had made the Musician go away, taking the music with him.

Cyrus had wanted him to find that letter.

So then *Cyrus* was the one he had to beat.

"This one's about *hope!*" Poppy called out from the other side of the room. "I know it!"

"What's about hope?" asked Azumi as she stepped away from Marcus and back toward the cupboards.

"This puzzle," said Poppy, placing three glass jars from the cupboard on the nearby circular table. "The one downstairs was about fear. This one's about hope." She stood and hopped giddily over the many jars that she and Dash and the other Azumi had placed on the floor. "Look at these three." One jar contained what looked like seeds. Another had a selection of variously colored seashells. The third was filled with blue eggshells. "They're the *only* ones that aren't filled with dead things. Scary-looking things." She shivered as she glanced

113

at the jars at her feet. "These are about growth. About birth. Happy things."

"Technically, seashells are dead," said long-haired Azumi.

A pounding came from the panel in the corner where the stairs were, followed a moment later by muffled howling. Everyone froze.

"They're getting angrier," short-haired Azumi said from where she knelt by the cupboard. "So are we going to test this out or what?"

Marcus bristled at the sound of her voice.

Poppy blinked back into herself. She slid the jars, one by one, to the center of the table, placing them onto the embossed circles. As the last one fit into place, something shifted in the wall behind the cupboard. There was a grinding noise, like stone moving against stone. "They're weighted just right!"

The cupboard split in two, right down the middle. A new opening revealed a hollow area in the wall behind it and a ladder that stretched up to the ceiling.

Short-haired Azumi leapt to her feet and threw her arms around Poppy. "This girl's a genius!" Poppy cringed at first, but then relaxed and hugged her back.

"Dylan?" called Dash. "You up there?"

Poppy pushed through the opening in the cupboard. As

114

she glanced back at everyone, Marcus could see the proud glint in her eye. Something about it made his stomach ache again. "Come on," said Poppy. "We don't have any time to waste."

"We also don't have any other options," Marcus muttered under his breath. He kicked at the scattered papers and gathered up the glass jars, placing them into the cupboard and mixing them back in with the others. He couldn't just leave them out for the Specials to find. He patted the page he'd tucked into the pocket of his jacket, and hurried after the others.

CHAPTER 21

IT'S DASH! **THINKS** Dylan. He wants to call out, *Wait for me!* But he holds his tongue.

The voices in the ceiling are starting to fade. However, Dylan's anger is just as strong as it's been since Del Larkspur scolded him and threatened to take away his role. For the past few minutes, Dylan has had to restrain himself from running back out the door and hiding in his dressing room, but he doesn't want the voice to scream at him again. If he makes it too angry, it'll be a long time before he gets to check in with Dash.

His cast members have made a mess of this room. The cat, the rabbit, and the bear. They've knocked over chairs and dragged the table toward the spot where the stairs disappeared into the ceiling. But Dylan says nothing. Del told him to follow the others from now on. The cat pauses before one of the bookshelves. Three taxidermied animals lie on the floor. A fox. A bobcat. A rabbit.

To his surprise, Dylan watches as the rabbit begins to squirm slightly, a soft wheezing escaping its mouth. The cat bends down and picks it up, holding it next to her pointed plastic ears. She nods as if the rabbit is whispering secrets.

The fox and the bobcat begin to shiver and shake. Dylan steps farther away, as if they might scurry toward him. The masked kids are silent now, so he keeps quiet too. He tries to adjust his mask so he can see better, but he finds that he can't move it, which scares him even more.

Where did Dash and the others go? Will they still be upstairs when he comes for them?

The girl in the cat mask stands and then arranges the squirming animals on the bookshelf so that they're standing upright. In the corner of the room, the stairs drop from the ceiling again. The trio of animal-faced kids begins to climb, but Dylan hangs back.

His longing to call out to his brother—to warn him maybe—grows stronger. Suddenly, Del's threat pops into his head: *Don't disappoint me again.*

Too late, says another voice in his ear.

An ache pounds at his temples, worse than before.

Dylan crouches, clutching his head. His vision blurs and his teeth chatter.

It's the mask, he thinks. *It's too tight.*

He needs air. He grabs at the mask and tries to pull it up and away, but his face moves with it, as if his skin is bonded to the plastic. He yanks harder. Pain tears through his skull. It feels like he's ripped his skin away from the muscle and cartilage underneath. He shrieks, releasing the mask, and then falls backward against the wall, struggling to catch his breath.

His three cast mates are watching from the stairs now, empty eyes revealing nothing.

"Help me!" he cries out. "Someone, please, get my brother!" Dylan rises and then stumbles toward them. And suddenly, somehow, he remembers.

Flash.

They attacked us! Me and Dash and Poppy and Marcus and Azumi. In the elevator, they tried to kill us! And in the music room, when we'd pulled away Randolph's dog mask, Marcus gave his harmonica to the boy and it set his spirit free from this place . . .

There had been no cameras watching. And if there had been a script, it had nothing to do with a movie.

But if that's true, Dylan realizes, then everything that Del told him earlier, about running lines and fainting, about the script he'd called *The Gathering* . . . It's all been a lie. There *is* no Del Larkspur. And Dylan's older visions, the ones about the dressing room on the set of *Dad's So Clueless*, about the bucket of water that had hit him, about the short-circuiting lamp he'd reached out to touch, about the morgue and the casket and the funeral . . . *those* had been the truth. The reality.

And that means Dylan actually *is*—

A knife blade of agony slices through his cranium again. He stumbles forward and falls to the floor.

The pain is the *clown mask's* fault—the mask that Del gave him. The mask that he cannot remove. Dylan knows that he's not in control anymore. But then, that means the other kids aren't in control either. They're chess pieces in a game.

The knife blade twists, as if someone is cutting open the top of his head. He's going to die, curled here on the floor of this room, shivering, just like he did the last time he—

Dylan smacks his forehead, again and again, until the offending thoughts scatter, running off into the shadowy parts of his brain.

CHAPTER 22

POPPY HELPED PULL Dash up from the ladder. He stood and brushed himself off, the last of the group to reach the third floor.

From below, there came a grinding noise. The cupboard slid shut, blocking them inside the new space.

This room was even gloomier than the last one. The walls and windows were painted black, and the only light came from bunches of tall white candles. Some sat squat on the floor. Others jutted up, long and skinny, from elaborate iron candelabras. The flames flickered, teasing the shadows.

"Someone must be close," whispered Poppy. "These candles can't have been burning for very long."

They could hear a scratching sound from down below. The Specials must have made it to the next room.

The kids huddled in the center of this new space, as if the person who'd lit the wicks might suddenly step out from the shadows. Their vision adjusted, and other details of the room came into focus. Dash glanced around, wondering if Dylan might somehow have been the one to leave the candles for them.

"This looks like the office I found on the second floor," Poppy went on. "The one that burst into flames when I tried to leave." She pointed toward several wooden filing cabinets hunched beside another desk. High stacks of papers were piled everywhere.

All Dash could think was: *Fire hazard.*

"Oh, that's so creepy," said Marcus, indicating five large photographs that were hanging side by side on one wall.

The Specials.

Their names were typed clearly on pieces of paper that were pinned to the bottom of each: Matilda. Esme. Aloysius. Irving. Randolph.

"Cyrus had *two* offices?" asked short-haired Azumi, stepping a little too close to her counterpart. The other girl practically leapt away.

Poppy's eyebrows lifted as she came to a realization. "That's why he set up these puzzles: to safeguard his darkest secrets."

"Okay," Marcus said, turning in the space. "Everyone look around. The key to getting out of here has got to be here somewhere."

Poppy sat down at the desk and tugged the thin folder at the top of the pile in front of her. Short-haired Azumi held a candle over the pages as they both started to read.

Inside, they discovered pages of dated notes, all of them signed by Cyrus. At the top of each was written a name: *Matilda Ribaldi.*

DAY ONE: GAVE M. THE FIRST DOLL. A PIONEER GIRL WITH A SIMPLE BROWN DRESS. M. IMMEDIATELY FELL IN LOVE. HUGGED IT LIKE IT WAS HER OWN CHILD. LATER, I HEARD M. RECITING FAIRY TALES TO IT. PERFECT.

DAY FOUR: CUT OFF THE PIONEER DOLL'S HAIR WHILE M. WAS SLEEPING. WHEN SHE WOKE, M. SCREAMED AND CRIED FOR NEARLY FIVE MINUTES. LATER, SHE COMFORTED THE DOLL, AS IF PART OF HER WERE LIVING INSIDE OF IT. TONIGHT, SHE READ TO IT GENTLY, LOVINGLY, AS IF NOTHING HAD HAPPENED.

DAY SEVEN: SMASHED THE PIONEER DOLL'S FACE DURING

BREAKFAST. M. SHRIEKED AT ME, CALLING ME A MONSTER. I
SHOWED NO EMOTION.

DAY EIGHT: FORCED M. TO WATCH AS I THREW THE
PIONEER GIRL INTO THE FIREPLACE. M. WAS SURPRISINGLY
RESTRAINED AS THE DOLL BURNED. SHE DIDN'T SAY A WORD TO
THE OTHER CHILDREN ABOUT IT. LATER, I HEARD HER TALKING
TO HERSELF IN HER BED. TELLING STORIES, AS IF THE DOLL
WERE STILL LISTENING. FASCINATING.

DAY NINE: GAVE M. THE SECOND DOLL. A PRINCESS IN A
RED BALL GOWN. AT FIRST, M. WAS HESITANT TO ACCEPT THE
GIFT. BUT WITHIN MINUTES, SHE APPEARED TO . . .

Poppy glanced at Azumi. "He was documenting it." Poppy
flipped through the rest of the pages. "Gross! The list goes on
and on. It's like he was keeping a record of how he broke
her. Evidence of his experiment."

Azumi held her hand to her mouth. "Poor thing," she
whispered.

At the back of the folder, Poppy noticed different handwriting on a new kind of paper. The date at the top caught
her attention. It was only from about five years prior to today.
Dear Ms. Tate, Please accept my apologies . . .

Ms. Tate?

Poppy's legs went numb. Ms. Tate was the director of Thursday's Hope, Poppy's group home. She glanced at the bottom of the letter. *Sincerely, Janis Caldwell.* The name there was a like a wallop to her jaw. The letter was from her mother! Poppy felt the room spin.

She scanned the rest of the letter quickly. Bits of it leapt out at her, sending a creeping chill across her body. *Never loved the child . . . Memories that make me want to do bad things . . . Her incessant crying . . . I don't trust myself . . . Please take her . . . Don't let her find me, ever . . .*

Poppy let out a small squeak before slamming her mouth shut and flipping the page over so she wouldn't have to see any more of it.

"What was that?" asked the short-haired Azumi.

Had Azumi read any of it? "I-I don't . . ." Poppy couldn't finish. Her throat felt tight, and she worried that if she tried to talk, she might throw up. Her fist closed on the paper, crumpling it into a tight wad.

Azumi slid over to the next folder. Taped inside were black-and-white photographs of a young girl whose face had been scratched away. "Esme had a sister she longed for, right?" Azumi asked. Her face reddened. "Like me. I wonder if this is a photograph of her?"

Poppy opened another folder. This time, the girls discovered pages and pages covered in what looked like red crayon: *SAY SOMETHING SAY SOMETHING SAY SOMETHING.*

"Aloysius," whispered Azumi. "The boy who didn't talk."

Poppy shook her head, her eyes stinging. Azumi rested her hand on Poppy's back. Azumi's fingers felt hot, like a cattle brand, and Poppy scooted away.

One thing was clear: Cyrus had wanted Poppy to find the letter from her mother. It wasn't enough for him to torture the orphans he'd brought to Larkspur. He'd pushed Matilda and Esme, Aloysius and the rest until they'd all cracked. It must have taken years. After seeing the horrible things in her mother's letter, Poppy was certain she wouldn't last nearly as long.

CHAPTER 23

DASH FORCED HIMSELF to ignore the whimpers and whispers coming from Poppy and one of the Azumis, huddled over the desk. Instead, he pretended to look closely at the photos of the Specials hanging on the walls. He couldn't stop thinking about his brother wandering these haunted hallways, encountering ghouls like the Foxes or the walking corpse from the greenhouse. Yes, *Dylan was dead*, but he wouldn't be if it hadn't been for the trick that Dash had played on him. He had found the others, and now he needed to find Dylan instead of poking around in a bunch of files. There was no way he could allow Cyrus to keep his brother trapped inside this nightmare.

"This is messed up," said long-haired Azumi. Reaching

into one of the filing cabinet drawers, she removed an ancient pair of leather shoes. She let them dangle from their laces for a moment, then dropped them to the floor with a heavy thump. She pulled another pair from the drawer. And another.

Poppy shifted away from the spot where she'd been reading. "Who did those belong to?" she asked, a weird tension creeping into her voice.

Where had her optimism gone? Dash wondered.

"Maybe to some of the orphans who lived here," said Marcus, leaning against a wall on the other side of the filing cabinets.

Almost manic, Poppy jumped to her feet. "What else is in these cabinets?" she asked. She started opening more of the drawers, practically shoving the long-haired Azumi aside.

"Look!" she said. She pulled out a headless doll, a jar filled with colorful hard candies, some torn sheet music, a deflated leather football, and a worn spiral-bound notebook with a pencil shoved into the spine. "Marcus is right! These line up with what we know about the Specials. Cyrus locked away whatever was left of their favorite possessions." Her face practically glowed with determination. "Now we just have to take off their masks and get these things to them."

"Can I see that last one?" asked short-haired Azumi. Poppy

held it out to her. The notebook was filled with scrawled letters. *Dear Sister* topped every page. "Esme," Azumi sighed. A leaf of paper slipped out from between the pages, and she scrambled to catch it. She took a glance at it, then screamed and tossed it away.

It fell to Dash's feet and he picked it up.

"Don't look at that!" Azumi cried out, reaching to snatch it back.

But he'd seen it. It was a crime scene photograph. A body was sprawled out on a forest floor, clothes dirty, but familiar. He'd seen them in the greenhouse downstairs.

"No!" screamed long-haired Azumi, catching a glimpse of it. "Moriko!" She rushed at Dash. Instinctively, he held up his hand. She bumped into him and bounced onto to the ground.

"Don't touch her!" shouted Marcus. He hurried to Azumi's side and helped her back to her feet.

Dash felt faint. "I didn't! She was trying to—"

"Just leave her alone," said Marcus, leading the sobbing, long-haired Azumi away from Dash.

"It-it's a picture of my sister," she said. "She's dead. She's really dead!" She broke down again, covering her face, as she shuddered and coughed. Marcus held her tight.

Short-haired Azumi squeezed into the space between

Poppy and Dash, looking pale but calm again. "She's faking it," she said in a flat voice. "I don't know why. But Marcus sure believes her."

"What was that photo doing in this filing cabinet anyway?" Dash asked.

Poppy spoke up. "It's just like . . ." She turned to look at Dash. "It's really weird . . . but I found a letter from my mom. It was in a folder—" Her voice hitched. "The letter said all of these horrible things about me."

Dash sniffed. "When I was alone in the greenhouse, I saw a piece of newspaper stuck to the window. It mentioned that the *police* are looking for me and that I was . . . I don't want to say what it said."

Poppy nodded. "Cyrus is messing with us," she said. "The letters and pictures and articles are simply more of his . . . *experiments*. He wants to hurt us. And keep hurting us. To see how much we can take." Poppy glanced toward Marcus and the other Azumi. "Are you guys listening? Marcus?"

Marcus nodded.

"Did you find anything?" Poppy asked. "A disturbing document, or something bad about your life from before you came to Larkspur?"

"No, nothing," said Marcus. He didn't meet her eyes. "But maybe I'm not like the rest of you."

"Well . . . maybe you're not," said Poppy, squinting as if she didn't believe him. "Maybe you're *special*."

"What are you hiding?" asked Dash quietly.

The scratching noises came from below again, followed by the sound of glass shattering. The cupboard!

Marcus's eyes went wide. He moved back toward the wall where he'd been standing earlier. There were indentations bored into the stone. As Dash came closer, Marcus began to climb.

"Marcus!" Poppy cried out. "Where are you going?"

"I think I see a hatch," Marcus said, his voice rising. "Maybe it's a way out." But when he reached the ceiling and pushed on the wooden panel over his head, it wouldn't move.

"What's that?" Dash called out. He reached up and pulled a small black notebook from the back of Marcus's khakis, holding it up.

"To be honest," said Marcus, climbing down, "I forgot I had it." He was chagrined. "It looks like it could be Cyrus's journal. He wrote about these plants called larkspur."

"*Larkspur?*" Poppy echoed, flipping the notebook open.

"Apparently it was his father's favorite flower," said long-haired Azumi, rubbing at the spot on her chin where the other Azumi had hit her. "There are two types: delphinium and consolida."

Poppy glanced up, her face paling.

"I know," said Marcus. "Like your cousin. Connie's parents must have named her after the flower."

"And *delphinium*," short-haired Azumi whispered. "*Delphinia . . . Del . . .*"

"If the house is a puzzle," said Poppy, "created by Cyrus to torture kids like us, then we *have* to look this over."

Dash reached for her shoulder. "Poppy, we're running out of time. Those kids could smash through—"

"This is important, Dash," she said, dropping to the floor, crossing her legs as she scooted closer to the nearby candle light.

"No!" he yelled, his anger rising up out of nowhere. Everyone jumped and looked at him as if he might explode. But Dash couldn't help himself. "*This* isn't what's important anymore. My brother needs me! Azumi's sister needs her—whichever of these two girls is the *actual* Azumi. We know that this house belonged to your family once upon a time. So what? Your great-great-great-cousin—or whoever!—was a

132

total psychopath? Who cares? Leave the past in the past! It's not helping us get what we need now. Which is to get out of this room!"

Everyone was silent for a moment, staring at him in shock.

"That's funny," Poppy answered moments later, "coming from you."

"Coming from me?" Dash echoed.

"*Leave the past in the past?*" Poppy exhaled slowly. "Dylan is dead, Dash. The rest of us aren't. *You* aren't."

Short-haired Azumi raised a hand. "Guys? Do you think that maybe this is exactly what Cyrus wants? We already know that fighting isn't going to get us anywhere." She blinked at Dash, as if her eyelashes could brush away whatever spell had just come over him. "Poppy got us out of the first two rooms. Why don't you just let her do what she needs to do?"

Dash clenched his fists and then turned as Poppy began to read, her voice shaking with anger and hurt.

CHAPTER 24

July 10, 1937. Yesterday, the children were laid down in the Larkspur mausoleum. Gage, Sybil, Eliza, James, and Orion. Rest in peace, children . . .

POPPY GLANCED UP from the notebook, swallowing back emotion. "Those were the names of the first orphans. The ones who drowned . . . and who tried to drown us while Cyrus swam to shore."

Short-haired Azumi sat beside her. "What a monster." Marcus and the other Azumi sat down a little farther away. Dash continued to wander around the rest of the room, still shaking with anger.

"This next one jumps ahead a few months," said Poppy,

134

continuing on. "*October 1, 1937. Bad memories are returning. Lately, I've seen the shadowy thing that haunted my childhood dreams lurking around the grounds. When I try to look at it straight on, it disappears. What does it want from me? I must do something before these thoughts drive me mad.*"

"Too late," Marcus added.

"I saw it this morning," whispered short-haired Azumi. "Remember? The thing that was chasing Poppy and Marcus across the meadow. It looked like . . . Well, I don't have words to describe it."

"*I* have words to describe it," said long-haired Azumi, crossing her arms. "Because *I* was the one who saw it this morning."

"Let's not start this again," said Poppy, glancing toward Dash, who was looking at a painting hanging in a far corner of the room. "Please. If you want us to trust either of you, just stop it."

"Sorry," said long-haired Azumi, slouching. Short-haired Azumi sighed, but she wouldn't take her eyes off her twin.

"There's more here," said Poppy. "A lot more."

"Tick-tock," Dash called out, glancing over his shoulder. "Come on, we need to find the next solution and get out!"

Poppy pressed her lips and then went on. "*December 31,*

135

1937. To my surprise, my maid, Rhona, brought me the most bizarre gift this afternoon: a page, written in my mother's hand, with a recipe of some unnamed tincture, which, it seems, is meant to ward off 'the presence of evil.'"

Poppy looked up. "Now, *this* is weird," she said, forcing her voice in Dash's direction. She continued to read. "*The main ingredient is a flower called larkspur, a poisonous plant that grows in the western states, where my father spent his youth. I have decided to write to Aunt Emily and see if she might procure some blossoms in the coming spring.*"

"I don't like this story," said the short-haired Azumi, scooting closer toward Poppy as if to protect herself from encroaching shadows.

"I don't either," said Dash. "Yes, it's weird. But so is everything in this house."

"*May 31, 1938*," Poppy read. "*The recipe worked! Something inside me has changed, and I feel like new. Like my father's Five-Sided Man, I now ascend when once I fell.*" She looked up again. "Five-Sided Man? What's a Five-Sided Man?" She shook her head. "*Why should I give up my dream of helping the unfortunate? I shall reopen the orphanage. I shall find new children. Better children. Larkspur will be reborn! The house will help me. We shall do this together.*"

"*Better* children?" said one of the Azumis. "What does that even mean?"

"I'm not sure," said Poppy. "But it doesn't sound good." She went on. "*January 7, 1939. Plans: 1. Seek out similar five. (Types: the Bookish Girl, the Musical Prodigy, the Sleepwalker, the Charismatic Boy, the Mute.) 2. Teach them my new 'method,' so that they understand what is to come and how they shall help me. 3. Find masks for them. 4. Keep them from sleep. 5. Reveal their phobias. 6. Deny them reward. 7. Discover boiling points. 8. Force them into* PSYCHIC BREAKS."

"*He* was the one who had a psychic break," said Marcus, trembling.

"*What did you do, Cyrus?*" Poppy continued to stare at the pages as if hypnotized.

"Five-Sided Man," said Dash, from the edge of the room. "*Five-Sided Man!* Hey, check out this painting. Looks like it might be a clue to another of Cyrus's puzzles."

The painting hung on the wall opposite from the ladder that Marcus had tried to climb, in a five-sided wooden frame. In its center, a man in an old-fashioned tuxedo was falling through an indigo sky, his head pointed toward the bottom of the frame, his legs together and his arms lifted slightly away from his body, palms facing up. His expression

was peaceful, as if he was resigned to plummet into infinity.

Poppy glared at Dash. "If we hadn't read the notebook, we wouldn't have realized he was important."

"Well, if *I'd* sat down and listened to your story," said Dash, "we wouldn't have even found the painting."

"Guys, this isn't a competition," said short-haired Azumi. "You know that, right?"

Poppy squinted back at the journal. "*Like my father's Five-Sided Man, I now ascend when once I fell*," she read. She looked at the painting. "Well, it looks like he's falling here."

"So maybe we need to make him ascend," said Marcus.

"How are we supposed to do that?" asked long-haired Azumi. "Paint a new painting?"

"It's easier than that," said Poppy, optimism creeping back into her voice. "Cyrus's puzzles all seem to center around opposites. Hope and fear. Falling and *ascension*." She grasped the frame and began to turn it. Something inside the wall began to shiver, the sound of a crank clicking slowly echoing from within. The others watched as the man on the canvas was turned over, his head pointed up instead of down. This simple change in perspective made it seem like he was no longer plummeting into darkness, but rising into the heavens.

"Whoa," said Dash.

Something rattled behind them. Looking up, the group watched as the hatch at the top of the ladder swung open with a *bang*. The darkness behind it seemed to inhale slightly as if trying to catch a whiff of them.

"Hello?" Poppy called out. But of course no one answered.

CHAPTER 25

POPPY HURRIEDLY GATHERED each of the Specials' treasures and Cyrus's journal into her pink messenger bag—if the Specials turned up again, she'd be ready with the exact thing each of them needed to be set free of Larkspur.

The next floor was windowless and very dark. Dozens of picture frames with blank canvas were propped at the base of the walls, leaning against one another. Glancing around, Poppy noticed a curved metal staircase hugging the circular wall. A small wooden cupboard sat just underneath it. At the top of the steps, an opening revealed a slice of evening sky and a few twinkling stars. Her heart began to pound. The way out!

When she reached the top of the staircase, the horizon

stretched all around her, and she realized how very high up she was. Except for a pitched wooden roof overhead, the top of the tower was open to the elements, the sky like an infinite indigo canvas with a smear of lighter blue to the west where the sun had set. A couple of the large picture frames leaned against the stone railing that enclosed the wide platform. The wind whipped Poppy's hair, and the world began to tilt. To stop herself from toppling over, Poppy grabbed on to the railing. Leaning forward, she saw Larkspur's roofline a couple of stories below—a series of sharp edges and spires and gables and glass. Catching her breath, she turned back toward the stairs to find that the rest of the group had caught up. The view entranced them all. The early evening light kept everyone in pale shadow. Their faces were like masks.

"I knew we should have gone to the greenhouse to find my sister," said short-haired Azumi. "You guys really want to climb down out *here*?"

"N-no," said Poppy, flustered.

"What was that?" Azumi went quiet. "I thought I heard something."

"*Something?*"

"A creak. Hinges. Like a door opening." She pointed at the stairwell. "Down there."

The group listened as the steps squealed under the weight of someone approaching.

"This is a dead end," whispered long-haired Azumi. "The Specials *wanted* us to come up here!" She shook her head, rubbing at her chin as if she could erase the red mark that the other Azumi had given her during the tussle downstairs, and then rushed to the closest railing. "There's no way down."

"We're prepared for them now," said Poppy, patting her bag and planting her feet.

Squeeeeeee . . . The stairs shook and rattled, and a shadowed head rose from the stairwell opening. Dash flicked his phone's light toward the silhouette. A very old man dressed in a ratty suit and dark jacket stared back. He had a sharp chin and prominent brow, sunken cheeks and thin lips, and electric eyes. Electric *eye*. Half of his face appeared to have been burned, covered by a great scar. His wild hair had turned white.

"Cyrus," Poppy whispered, her voice a mouse squeak as he swept toward them.

He focused his gaze on her, and his eye glinted with satisfaction. "P-Poppy," he croaked, his hand twitching as it pointed at her, "you've found your way to m-m-me."

CHAPTER 26

"EVERYBODY . . . GET BACK!" Marcus shouted, holding out his arms to shield his companions. "We don't know what he's capable of."

To their surprise, the old man laughed. His spine twisted momentarily before straightening again, and he muttered quickly, as if he were trying to block out voices in his head. After a moment, he replied softly, "D-do I look capable of *anything* anymore?"

He was practically a walking skeleton. Skin sagged from his face as if he were an ancient creature—maybe the oldest man Poppy had ever seen—a frail, fragile, broken *thing*. Then the letter from her mother flashed into Poppy's head, like a paper cut across her brain.

"Stop lying to us," Marcus said. But Cyrus stepped toward the group.

Dash yelled, "Don't you move!"

Cyrus lifted his palms. "I know what you all must think of me," he replied. "But I am *the only one* who knows the way out of this house. And I promise you, I want to help."

"If you know the way out of this house," asked Marcus, "then why are you still here?"

"Oh, *I* can't leave. I would if I could. But it won't let me."

Poppy shivered. "*What* won't let you?"

Cyrus squinted, his neck twitching, jerking his skull briefly back and forth. "Y-you already know the answer to that."

Was this what the "first orphans" had meant to do? wondered Marcus. Send them all into the tower to meet Cyrus? Had they been on his side the whole time? Had he managed to twist *them* too?

"I cannot tell you that I am a good man," said Cyrus, "for I am not. I have d-done things—horrid things—things I'd n-never imagined . . . But you don't understand that I was under the influence of something far stronger than me."

"You're lying!" Marcus cried out again. "Everything you've done, you've done because you're—you're *evil*!"

145

"Oh, how I w-wish it were that simple," Cyrus answered, his eyes growing dark with memory.

We have a job to do, thinks Dylan. *We have a job to do. A job to do.*

The cat girl finally places three jars on the table, and the cupboard splits in two.

He climbs through the tower, following the masked kids, sensing the others who've come before them. There will be a battle. Soon. *A job to do . . .*

Voices echo from above. The old man. He's talking with a different group. Telling them what to do. *Giving them their own jobs . . .*

The pain has finally gone away. Dylan is tempted to think about the past, about a brother—does he have a brother?—but he's learned to not do that anymore. He's the Trickster. He *is* the Trickster. Who else would he be? The mask feels tight, and it itches, but he knows now that there's nothing he can do about that. The others had been right. Best to not fight. Best not to—

The cat girl raises a hand, stopping them at the bottom of the next ladder. *Listen*, she whispers.

Dylan chuckles, thinking that it's funny how her voice came from inside his own head.

Listen . . .

CHAPTER 27

"IT TOOK YEARS of searching," said Cyrus, "but then, it seemed like I found the new five all at once. M-most of them weren't even orphans. But that didn't matter to me. The creature told me that the new children should be similar to the first ones. So I found a way to get them here."

Poppy interrupted, "What do you mean, *the creature*?"

Cyrus focused his eye on her, and she cringed away from him. "It's the . . . intelligence that rules this place. Everything you've seen. Everything you've heard. The m-messages, the letters, the articles, the photographs. I had n-nothing to do with any of it."

Words from the horrible letter sliced through Poppy's

mind. *Never loved the child . . . Don't let her find me, ever . . .*

"You mean, my mother never said those things?"

"The newspaper wasn't real?" asked Dash.

Cyrus shook his head.

"I want to believe you," said short-haired Azumi, hands folded, as if trying to look polite. "But after everything we've seen"—she glanced at the other Azumi—"how can you expect us to?"

But part of Poppy *did* believe him.

Cyrus paused for a moment, his breath hitching as if something was choking him. "T-the creature wants to feed on you. On your energy, on your fear. You will keep it alive for the next dozen or so years, until it can lure another five children. It's a pattern I've watched helplessly for decades. It twists your memories and plays with your weaknesses, causing what I once referred to as a *psychic break*." His voice wobbled. "W-what I did to those kids . . . Somehow, I thought I was doing *g-good*! H-helping them overcome whatever was holding them back!"

Cyrus covered his face and sobbed, his shoulders heaving.

"This is insane," said long-haired Azumi, grabbing Marcus's wrist. "How can we believe anything he's saying?"

"She's right," said Marcus. "There's no way of knowing the truth."

148

But Poppy kept her eyes on Cyrus. "Just . . . let me think."

"It doesn't add up," said Dash. "I think we should—"

"What about my sister?" asked short-haired Azumi. "She's waiting for us in the greenhouse."

Long-haired Azumi spat out, "Yeah, like we're ever going to find our way back—"

"I can prove myself," said Cyrus. "Y-you all have questions, do you not? L-little things that haven't added up over the p-past hours. In the elevator, did you not notice that only four of the five Special children appeared from the darkness to attack you? Where was the *other one*? The g-girl in the chimpanzee mask?"

The group looked at one another, the idea blooming in their heads at once.

"*One of you is not who you claim to be*," Cyrus went on. He reached for the long-haired Azumi, who was still rubbing at her chin. She leapt away, and Marcus jumped in front of her. "Don't go near her!" he shouted at Cyrus, eyes wild.

But before anyone else could move to protect her, Azumi thrust her fist into Cyrus's chest. He flew backward, stumbling toward the railing as Azumi turned toward the group and smiled, proud of herself.

There was a scrabbling sound as the Specials climbed up to the top of the tower at last.

CHAPTER 28

EMERGING FROM THE stairwell, a girl in a gray uniform and a cat mask stepped toward the group, followed by two more masked figures. Or was it three? Cyrus shouted out as two of the masked children grabbed him, holding him still.

"Azumi?" Marcus whimpered. "How . . . how did you do that?"

She stared at him, but only continued to smile.

Everyone watched as long-haired Azumi's eyes seemed to grow and the sides of her mouth began to droop in an exaggerated frown. The girl hitched a breath as a patch of skin crumbled away from her chin, revealing something hard and dark underneath.

Fighting nausea, Poppy covered her mouth. Marcus leaned

against the railing, his mind reeling, horrified by the girl's sudden transformation.

Soon, the gray patch had spread across the girl's face. Her skin cracked, like broken papier-mâché, and then began to rain to the floor in small clumps. The breeze whipped pieces of it away, off the roof.

A glass vial filled with a dark liquid dropped to the floor with a clink.

"Esme," whispered Poppy. A girl in a chimp mask glared back at them.

Marcus moaned as if someone had just punched him in the stomach.

"I was telling you the truth, Marcus," said Azumi—the real Azumi—wiping away angry tears. "*She* was the one who lied."

Poppy stammered, unable to form thoughts. There was something she had to do . . . Her bag! Shaking, she dug through the items from the filing cabinet. Her hand brushed against hard candies, the soft leather football, and the spine of a spiral notebook. *Esme's* notebook. "Azumi!" Poppy cried, pulling the notebook from the bag. "Catch!" And then she threw the book across the landing.

Azumi caught it, clapping it between her palms and

holding it away from herself awkwardly. "What do I do with it?" she asked.

Cyrus let out a yelp as the Specials dragged him along the railing. Poppy stepped forward, reaching out to him as if she could help, but Matilda jumped out and swiped at her. Irving climbed onto Cyrus's back, swinging the chains that joined his ankles up around the old man's torso. Cyrus grunted, struggling to stand upright as Aloysius shoved at his chest again and again.

Esme threw back her head and laughed. Then she lunged at Marcus. He dodged her and then cried out, "Poppy! Help!" To his shock, Poppy rushed toward Cyrus instead. "*Poppy!*" Esme clutched his jacket.

Poppy grasped at Aloysius's rabbit mask, but he shook her off. She fell back and Aloysius landed a blow that doubled Cyrus over. Irving fell to the floor.

Furious, Marcus yanked himself out of Esme's grip and rolled closer to the corner where Azumi stood, frozen.

Dash tried to skirt the cat girl, to make it back toward Azumi too, but the cat snarled and leaned toward him, threatening to charge.

"The mask!" Dash shouted, ducking Matilda's fist. "Azumi, you have to take off Esme's mask!"

The girl in the chimp mask lunged for Azumi, but Azumi leaned in to the attack, reaching her arms around Esme. She hugged her with one arm, and with the other, she raked her fingers across the chimp mask, catching the end and tossing it over the railing. Esme gasped and went rigid. Azumi took a small step back and looked up into the eyes of the dark-haired girl standing before her. They were filled with fear and confusion.

The other Specials stopped what they were doing, staring in awe.

Cyrus slumped against the railing, struggling for breath, barely able to move.

"Give her the notebook, Azumi!" said Poppy.

"I . . . I'm so sorry for what I did to you," said Esme, her voice hoarse. "I tried to stop it. I really did. But this place . . . Don't trust *anyone*. Not even yourself."

Azumi didn't know how to answer. Panting, she shoved the notebook into Esme's hands.

A grin blossomed on Esme's face. She flipped the notebook open, gasping at the handwriting she'd placed there decades earlier. *Dear Sister . . .* She turned page after page, her smile growing wider. Then, hugging the book to her chest so tightly she almost buried herself in it, she started to fade away, just as

Randolph had done when Marcus had given him the harmonica. Colors leached from her body, like watercolor paint from wet paper, and soon, all that was left of her was a bit of soft laughter. Before Azumi could say good-bye, the wind had taken that away too.

Matilda howled in frustration, snapping the other Specials back into action. She and Aloysius turned toward Cyrus. Black goo dribbled from the rabbit mask, and the old man sputtered and moaned. The cat girl rushed forward as Aloysius shoved Cyrus again toward the edge of the tower.

"Stop!" cried Poppy. "Leave him alone!" But even as she pushed away from the wall, her bag snagged on one of the empty gilt frames, and she tripped, landing hard on her side.

She saw movement out of the corner of her eye, and the noise of the brawl quieted as a girl appeared, impossibly, on the canvas. It was Poppy's Girl—her cousin, Connie Caldwell—though she flickered in and out of focus, and her expression was pained, as if it took tremendous effort to be there at all.

She reached out her hands to Poppy, like she had in the mirror at Thursday's Hope so many times, but this time, instead of a strange object, she held a small black notebook. Cyrus's journal!

"Is that what he needs?" Poppy gasped.

But Connie was gone.

Irving saw the notebook in Poppy's hands and lurched over to Cyrus before she could get there, climbing the railing and looping the chains from around his ankle over the old man's neck.

"Nooo!" Poppy screamed, jumping up and thrusting the journal into Cyrus's hands. He looked down in awe, for just a second, until his feet slipped out from under him. Irving, Aloysius, and Cyrus tumbled over the railing together and disappeared, screaming as they fell.

CHAPTER 29

THE AIR GREW still. Dash clutched at his scalp. And that's when he noticed another kid watching from the top of the stairs. This new kid was wearing a mask too—the sad clown who'd chased him through the hallway. Who was he?

Matilda rushed over to the boy and took his hand.

Besides the red-and-black shirt he wore, the clown-faced boy was dressed in the exact same clothes that Dylan had been wearing earlier. A T-shirt. Shorts. Sandals.

Dash's stomach flipped. No, this had to be another trick. Just like what the house had done with Esme, how it had made her appear as Azumi, just to mess with everyone, to scare them and confuse them. To give Dash hope before whisking it away again.

Matilda and the boy slipped quickly back down the stairs, as if they might save Aloysius and Irving somehow.

"Wait!" Dash called out. Poppy grabbed on to his shoulder before he could follow them. "*Dylan*," he said to her. "I think he was one of them. He was wearing that creepy clown mask. They're getting away. *She* has him!"

Poppy turned to Azumi and Marcus, who were cowering against the far railing. "Stay here. We'll be right back."

Dash didn't wait for an answer. He hurried down into the darkness.

"Poppy!" Azumi screamed.

Poppy looked over her shoulder at Azumi. "I have to go. I made a promise."

A moment later, Poppy was gone.

A sudden wind whipped harshly through the balcony.

"I didn't know who to believe," said Marcus. Azumi skidded away from him, shaking her head. "It was a trick. She tricked me! You know what that feels like. You were part of it. She looked just like you!"

"Marcus, stop talking," said Azumi, holding up her hand as if that could keep him at bay. "I don't want to hear your voice anymore."

A damp warmth coated Marcus's cheeks. He touched his face and realized that he was crying. "I'm so sorry. Please."

Azumi shuddered and then stood, glancing toward the stairs that Dash and Poppy had descended. "I can't believe they left us. I can't believe they followed those awful Specials." Looking at Marcus, she said, "All of you are just so . . ."

"We're scared," said Marcus. "Fear makes you do stupid things."

"It makes *you* do stupid things," said Azumi. "Really stupid things." She glanced around, taking in the darkening horizon. "I'm not staying here." She released a slow, shaky breath, and then rubbed at her arms, bending her elbows and stretching her shoulders as if gauging her level of pain. "So which would be stupider: going after Poppy and Dash, or climbing down this tower?"

"You seriously want my opinion?" asked Marcus. Azumi nodded, her face a blank slate. "I think climbing down the tower would be a really bad idea right now."

"I agree," said Azumi. She grasped the edge of the railing and slung one leg and then the other over, clinging to the outside edge of the balcony.

"Azumi, what are you doing?!" Marcus cried out.

"Getting away from you," she said, and then began to lower herself down the precipice.

Dash and Poppy reached the floor of the gallery as Matilda slipped beneath the floor's hatch. Candlelight flickered up through the hole, painting an abstracted rectangle on the wall to their right. Around them, the familiar pulsing sound echoed softly from Frederick's empty frames. *Whump-whump. Whump-whump. Whump-whump.*

A floorboard creaked across the room, and Dash and Poppy paused, looking back.

The boy in the clown mask stepped forward. Dash held up his phone, shining the flashlight at him. "You shouldn't be here," said the boy. The voice was muffled, but there was something else about it that made Dash wonder if someone other than his brother was using it to speak through Dylan's mouth. "You're going to ruin the scene."

"Dylan," said Dash, trying to keep his voice from trembling. "We've been looking everywhere for you. Why are you wearing that?"

"For the movie, dum-dum." Dylan chuckled. "You couldn't find me. But I've been watching you. Pretty funny when I grabbed your leg and you fell down those steps. You almost made it look real."

"*You* did that to him?" asked Poppy.

"The director really liked it," said Dylan. "He wants more."

"You hurt me!" Dash raised his crutch to show Dylan. "I busted up my arms and twisted my ankle!"

"I could've made it look *better* than that," said Dylan. "But you have your role now, and I have mine."

"Why are you acting like this?" asked Dash. "I get that you're mad at me, but—"

"Mad at you?" The clown mask tilted. "Why would I be mad at you?"

Dash pressed his lips together, afraid to answer, afraid to bring back the memories from the dressing room accident.

Poppy stepped forward. "Dylan, come up to the balcony with us. It's not safe here."

"You got that right," said Dylan.

"What do you mean?"

Dylan came closer. "We didn't like it when the old man was talking to you. He's not supposed to tell. And you shouldn't listen." His voice growled out from behind the clown's wide dark frown. He sprinted toward them, hands clenched into fists.

Poppy ducked the blow, but Dash leaned in to it, as if to knock Dylan off-balance. His crutch dropped to the floor. Dylan's forearm caught Dash's throat, and then Dash dropped too. Dylan pounced, grinding his knee into his brother's back. Dash screamed. Poppy lurched and shoved at Dylan's side, but it was like hitting at a small boulder.

"The mask, Poppy!" yelled Dash, his face smashed into the floor. "Get it off him."

Poppy pressed her fingers into the hollow gap just below Dylan's jawline, but he jerked away. Her grip slipped, and she flew backward, rolling toward the open hatch. Imagining Matilda coming up to claw at her, she scooted against the wall, away from the fighting twins.

Still crushing Dash's back with his knee, Dylan glanced at her. *"Boo-hoo-hoo,"* he said, followed by a fake, almost-mocking wail. *"My mask is stuck. Take it off me, Dash. Take it off! What am I going to doooo?"* He twisted his knee, screaming a high-pitched cackle.

Dash groaned. "Poppy, help!" He reached out to her as Dylan pounded his elbow into Dash's shoulder. *"Auuggh!"* he shouted in pain.

As Poppy scrambled to her feet, her hand brushed against the crutch lying on the floor. She picked it up and swung it at Dylan.

Wham!

The impact sent shivers up Poppy's arms, and Dylan flew off his brother's back, landing several feet away.

"Poppy!" Dash croaked, rolling over to stare at his brother's limp body. "What did you do?"

"I-I helped." She rushed to Dash and propped one of his arms over her shoulder. "I'm sorry. He was going to . . ." Then she rose, bringing him up with her. She handed him the crutch. Dash winced as he leaned on it. "I didn't know what he was going to do to you."

Dash caught his breath as he peered at Dylan, not wanting to get too close. "He's not okay."

"In more ways than one," Poppy whispered. "What now?"

Dash limped over and then bent down. He plucked the mask away from Dylan's face. His brother was flat on his back, glassy eyes staring up at the ceiling. "Dylan, I'm so sorry," said Dash, his breath ragged. His fingertips felt numb, and he tossed the mask into a dark corner of the room.

Dylan stirred; his arms shifted and his knees bent slightly.

His eyes focused on Dash. Then they grew wide with recognition, filling with tears. "Dash? Is that you?"

Dash tried to lean toward his brother, but Poppy clung to his elbow, forcing him to keep still. "Yes, it's me," said Dash, trying not to choke as his throat clenched with guilt. "Are you all right?"

"Everything hurts," said Dylan, trying to sit up. "Where are we?"

"We're still in Larkspur. But we're going to get you out."

"You have to come with us, Dylan," said Poppy. "Do you think you can stand?"

"Thank you," said Dylan. "I knew you'd find me, Dash. I knew you'd never leave me alone. I've been so scared. This house, it's . . . it's a bad place."

"We know," said Dash, extending his hand. "We've just started to understand exactly *how* bad it is."

Dylan reached out and squeezed Dash's wrist. "You know the way out? There's an exit?"

"The important thing right now is to get you away from the Specials," said Poppy. "They did something to you, but we're going to fix it."

"You're going to fix me?" asked Dylan, still clinging to his brother's wrist. "You really think you can do that?"

"Ow," said Dash. "You're squeezing too hard."

"Oh! I'm sorry!" said Dylan said. But then he released a laugh so low and languorous that it chilled Poppy's bones.

"Let go of me!" shouted Dash, tensing with panic, like an animal caught in a hunter's snare.

Dylan glared at them. "You think you can fix me? Erase the past? Start fresh?" He chuckled again. His eyes were dim and almost gray. It was not Dylan staring at them now, but something else. "After what *you* did? You're so clueless. You have no idea what's going on here."

Poppy pulled at Dash's shoulders as he yanked himself backward, freeing himself from Dylan's grasp. "No, Dylan," Dash whispered. "No, no, no."

Dylan's mouth began to droop, his skin changing into the artificial white of the clown's makeup. His eyes sank back into his skull, turning into pitch-black pools. "But don't worry," Dylan added. "You'll learn soon enough."

"Don't come near us!" said Poppy. "Please!"

Dylan rose to his feet and stepped toward them. "But I thought you were going to fix me. *Fix me*, Dash. I need you, little brother."

Dash held up his crutch, poking Dylan toward the hole in the floor.

"Dash . . . No . . . Please! What are you doing?"

Poppy grabbed Dash's arm and shoved it forward, knocking the crutch into Dylan's chest. Dylan fell backward, his feet scrambling at the edge of the hatch, and he was gone. A crash echoed out from below, followed by a harsh scream.

"Dylan!" Dash cried.

"He was going to hurt you," said Poppy. "And we don't know what it is that he needs. Not yet."

"He's broken," said Dash, leaning on his crutch.

"This is just a setback," said Poppy. "We can still help him."

"But how?" asked Dash. "I knew . . . *I knew*—ever since I fell down the stairs—that it was Dylan who tripped me. It was Dylan who laughed. It was Dylan who chased me and Azumi through that hallway, to the door with the nails in it. I didn't want to believe, but Moriko was right. Something in this house has twisted my brother. He's had a *psychic break*. Maybe it's happening to all of us. Maybe it's *already* happened."

Poppy shook her head, but Dash rushed on, "I was so horrible to you downstairs! The things I said . . . It wasn't fair. I just felt so much . . . rage. That's not who I want to be."

"Then don't be that person anymore," said Poppy, taking his hand. "Just because something is broken doesn't mean it can't be put back together again."

There was a scuffling noise from below, and Poppy hurriedly flipped the hatch shut, hoping it would give them even a tiny head start.

She and Dash turned away from where Dylan had fallen and raced toward the staircase back up to the balcony.

CHAPTER 30

"THEY'RE COMING!" POPPY shouted as she stepped back onto the rooftop. But when she looked around, she realized that Marcus and Azumi were gone.

"Do you think they jumped?" asked Dash, swiping away the tears and blood that had gathered just above his lip.

"Jump? They'd have to be—" *Crazy* . . . Poppy flew toward the railing that faced the river. The ground below seemed very far away—much higher than the five stories they'd climbed. Nobody was down there, not even Cyrus. "Where did they go?"

A commotion rang out from behind them—the hatch a floor below burst open.

"Poppy, we need to move!"

Without thinking, Poppy lifted herself up onto the stone railing. It was just wide enough for her to find her balance. She reached down to help Dash with his crutch. They stood together on a few inches of ledge, at the highest point in Larkspur, nothing behind them but air, nothing protecting them from a fall. The stars seemed to throb overhead in time with the beating of Poppy's heart. She closed her eyes and bent her knees. *Consolida*, she thought, *please protect us.*

"*Poppy!*" A voice echoed into the evening. Poppy froze, clinging to Dash's arm. "*Over here!*"

The voice seemed to be coming from their right. Edging to the corner of the railing, Poppy glanced down and saw Larkspur's pitched slate roof just two levels below. Azumi was crouched beside Marcus, who was clutching his knee. The two were perched inside a crevice where one of the gabled windows met the roof. "Be careful!" Azumi called. "Marcus fell. He hurt himself really bad!"

Poppy felt her stomach twist.

From the staircase there came a sudden crash, followed by the groaning of the iron steps as bodies barreled upward. The Specials burst out onto the rooftop again like wildcats released from a cage. Matilda had found Irving and Aloysius.

"Oh, no!" said Dash.

Poppy felt the messenger bag swaying at her side. "Do we fight them?"

"I don't think I can," said Dash. "My ankle—"

"Lower yourselves down," Azumi called to them. "Quickly!"

The Specials paused by the stairs, as if they were waiting for something. Then Poppy gasped as Dylan came slowly up the stairs behind them, his clown mask in place, his shoulders squared as if he was refreshed, ready for war. He was one of the Specials now. The whole group zeroed in on Poppy and Dash, their plastic faces turning as one, their hollow eyes like pits.

Poppy screamed.

Dash cried out, "Leave us alone!"

"The stonework is like a ladder!" said Azumi. "You can do it!"

"O-okay," Poppy choked out. She and Dash lowered themselves down, looking for the next outcroppings they could step on. Footfalls rang out as the Specials and Dylan rushed toward them from across the balcony. A gust of wind nearly knocked Poppy off-balance, and she clung more tightly to the base of the railing's stone posts.

Then the cat mask appeared, pressed into the space between the posts right in front of Poppy. Matilda reached through, her fingernails swiping at Poppy's face.

"Careful!" Dash shouted.

Poppy slipped down, catching herself on an ornamental ledge a couple of feet below, pressing her body against the stone wall. When Dash did the same, the crutch fell from his grip. It flew away, twisting in the wind, before disappearing around the side of the tower.

Glancing up, Poppy saw Matilda, Aloysius, Irving, and Dylan climbing over the railing. They weren't going to stop. They *couldn't* stop, she knew. Something in the house wouldn't let them.

"There's another ledge a few feet below the one you're on," called out Azumi. "Be careful, but hurry!"

"Can you make it?" Poppy asked Dash.

Dash's face was contorted with pain. "I'll try."

Poppy held on to the stonework with one hand and helped Dash down to the next ledge with the other, trying not to get tangled in the messenger bag that still looped across her chest. When Dash made it, he balanced on his good leg and reached up to guide her down too.

"Only a little bit farther," called Azumi.

Poppy looked up. The Specials were already helping one another climb the space just above them. Matilda whipped her head down to face her.

"Dylan!" Dash cried out to the group overhead. "I know you can hear me! Fight it. Whatever it is. You're stronger than this!"

But Dylan threw back his head and chortled. Matilda shook her head pityingly at Poppy and Dash.

"Please," Poppy said, her voice barely rising over the wind. "We want to *help* you. Just like we did for Randolph. And for Esme. You can be free too!" Poppy thought of the moment when she'd first removed Matilda's mask in the elevator, of the girl's surprise, which was apparent in her bright blue eyes. She remembered talking to her in the music room, gaining the first hint that the house's foundations might have cracks, that there might be a way to actually beat away the evil that lived here. But then Matilda's mask had reappeared, and she ran off, back under the control of Cyrus, or Larkspur.

Matilda pulled one of her monstrous dolls from a pocket in her uniform and waved it at Poppy. Its ceramic face was smashed open. It was bald and naked, and it looked heavy. She held out her hand and released the doll.

It dropped quickly, smacking Poppy's shoulder, knocking

her off-balance. Poppy swung her arms out, as if she could flap back to safety, but she felt herself tipping away from the building.

Dash tried to grab at her T-shirt, but he only managed to get his fingertips on the bottom of the hem as Poppy tumbled off the ledge. And that was enough to pull him forward too.

The pitched roof rushed toward them from below.

CHAPTER 31

DASH LANDED ON his back. Pain erupted in his rib cage, like nothing he'd ever felt before. When he tried to catch a breath, it felt as though his lungs had evaporated. Slowly, slowly, the air crept down his throat, its crispness shocking him back into the world.

He was alive at least. Wasn't he? He couldn't be sure of that anymore.

Poppy had fallen beside him. She was rigid with pain, her head cradled in her hands.

Above, the stars glared down. The sky was filled with constellations that Dash didn't recognize from the textbooks he and Dylan had studied on set. He felt the sloping roof beneath him begin to shift, and he realized that both he and Poppy had started to slip.

They slid faster and faster toward the sharp line of the roof edge. Poppy cried out and flailed her arms and legs, searching for something to grab on to, but she only managed to clasp Dash's shirt. He pressed his hands down flat on the roof, to try to slow them, but the slate was slick, and every bump they hit seemed to hurry them toward the green copper gutter. "Hold on, Poppy!" he shouted. "I'm going to try and grab—"

Just then, Dash felt a sharp yank at his collar, and together, he and Poppy arced across the slope, just missing the drop. She had her arms wrapped around his waist, stretching his spine. Their momentum slowed and then stopped. He choked as the cotton collar squeezed his windpipe. But then he felt someone clasp his forearms and pull. Looking up, he saw Azumi, her face red as she strained against his weight. Marcus was crouched beside her in the nook of the gabled window, holding Dash's shirt in his fist. "Can't . . . breathe!" Dash managed.

"Sorry!" said Marcus, giving him some slack.

"You take Dash," Azumi said to Marcus. "I'll grab Poppy."

Marcus helped Dash climb forward as Azumi pulled Poppy to safety.

The Specials were still up on the tower, watching them. Dash wondered how long they'd stay there.

"Are you hurt?" asked Azumi.

"I don't think so," said Poppy, settling into the nook above the gabled roof. Somehow, the pink messenger bag was still looped across her chest.

Dash's palms stung, scraped raw during the slide. His forearms and his ankle continued to ache. And the spot on his back where Dylan had elbowed him throbbed. "I'll live," he whispered, his voice still weak.

"Which way do we go?" asked Azumi.

Marcus nodded toward the edge of the roof several yards away. "Maybe we can keep climbing down from here."

"We're still at least three floors up," said Poppy. "What if we slip again?"

Azumi pointed away from the tower, where the spine of the roof shot off into the dark. "I think the roof slopes in that direction. We'll be closer to the ground."

"Yes," said Poppy. "Then we run for the driveway. The gate is down the path through the woods."

"Guys!" Dash shouted. "We have to go! Now!" He pointed at the tower.

They all turned just in time to watch the four Specials leap from the ledge. *Wham!*

The Specials hit near the peak by the tower wall and then disappeared, slipping down the other side. Several pieces of slate tiles broke off and slid—*clink, clank, clink, clank*—before falling over the edge a few feet away.

Dash, Poppy, Azumi, and Marcus lurched to their feet. They held hands and slowly made their way up the slope, moving away from the tower and the Specials. When they reached the ridge of the roof, Dash glanced over his shoulder. The Specials and his brother were only several dozen feet back, rising crooked and broken to their feet. They turned to look at the group, as if they sensed his gaze.

Dash cried out, "Go! Go! Go!" He pushed the others ahead of himself, limping along as quickly as he could.

Azumi had been right. Here, the roof pitched downward at a steep degree. Only a handful of yards stood between them and what looked like a one-story drop down to the ground. The pitter-patter of sliding tiles rang out from behind them, but no one dared to look back.

As Dash limped along, his arm slumped across Poppy's

shoulders, his mind was racing, tripping through time. He thought of his brother, of the accident, the guilt he'd carried all the way across the country. Dash pushed himself to go faster, ignoring the pain that shot through his ankle, not because he was afraid that the Specials were gaining on them—they were—but because he finally understood that maybe Dylan was actually unreachable.

The others were moving just as quickly. There appeared to be only a hundred more feet until they reached the edge of the house. The Specials howled and screamed, their muffled voices growing louder as they careered closer. Dash thought he felt a sharp fingernail scratch at his spine, and a yelp escaped his throat.

But then, a strange thing happened. The footsteps behind them halted. The Specials' cries went silent.

Everyone slowed. At the same time, the roof beneath their feet started cracking and squeaking like ice over a frozen pond.

Several steps ahead, Azumi and Marcus skidded to a stop. Dash and Poppy did the same. "What are they doing?" asked Poppy.

Dash turned back. The four masked kids had halted farther up the slope. The roof looked strange at the place where they'd paused. And then Dash realized why they'd stopped. The roof there was still slate. But farther along, where Dash and Poppy and Azumi and Marcus were now standing, the surface of the roof reflected the stars above them. Little points of white light sparkled all around their feet, as if the group was floating, weightless, in the sky.

"Oh, no," said Poppy, looking down. Her own face stared back darkly. "Are we standing on *glass*?" For a moment, there was a strange blur in the reflection below. It looked as though another person were standing beside Poppy, shivering and shaking and jerking like mad. "Connie?" she whispered, her voice a squeak. "Is that you?"

Dash glanced at Azumi. The surface shuddered and then shrieked. They both managed to say, "The greenhouse," right at the moment the roof shattered and the house swallowed them up.

CHAPTER 32

GLASS RAINED ALL around in huge chunks like great, dangerous icicles, and in little flecks that tinkled to the ground like sleet.

Azumi was draped on a high branch in a gnarled tree, her arms dangling down on one side, her legs on the other. It felt like someone had slammed a two-by-four into her gut. She could barely move, barely think, never mind call out and ask if everyone else was okay.

Careful to not make a sound, Azumi pulled herself up onto the branch. Glancing around, she took in the wide hole in the ceiling several dozen feet overhead and the speckled sky beyond. Near the edge of the hole, a large piece of glass—bigger than the stones on the path below—was hanging precariously from a thin piece of the bent metal frame. Looking down, she couldn't make out the others.

If the fall didn't kill them, she thought, *then the shards of glass—*

She remembered the phone in the pocket of her denim jacket. Pulling it out, she swiped on the light, and then scanned the area below her. Using branches near the trunk, she lowered herself through the canopy. With each step, more of the forest floor was revealed—rippled and rocky and covered with carpets of green moss that seemed to glow in an odd way whenever her light hit it.

Azumi froze. There was a body! It was lying on the ground just beneath her, cradled in a pocket of earth created by one of the tree roots. Red hair. Khaki pants. Marcus! She wanted to shout out to him, but remembered what lived in the greenhouse and managed to hold it inside. She scrambled the rest of the way down the tree and rushed to his side.

"Marcus," she whispered, pressing her fingertip to his cheek. He flinched, and she yelped in both surprise and relief, her voice echoing briefly through the woods. "You're okay," she told him, though she knew she might have also been talking to herself. "You're okay. *You're going to be okay.*"

Marcus curled his shoulder away from her touch and

then mumbled, "But, Mom, it's the weekend. I don't want to get up yet."

Azumi pressed her lips together to keep from laughing. It wasn't even that funny. Her adrenaline was pumping, making her woozy. She shook him hard, whispering in his ear. "*I'm not your mother.*"

Marcus's eyes flashed open, as if he was waking from a nightmare. He looked at her and then scrambled to sit up, but when he bumped his knee against the trunk, he yelled out, "Oww!"

"Shh! We're not alone in here."

"In here?" he repeated. "*In* where? We're outside."

"We're not," she whispered. "We fell. Remember? The roof caved in. We're in the greenhouse. Well . . . sort of."

"What do you mean, *sort of*?"

"It's hard to explain."

"No," he yelled, looking around but finding only darkness. "No! We got out of the house. We escaped!"

"Keep it down, you idiot!" Azumi said.

"No! We got out! This is . . . just a dream! We're dreaming, right?"

She reached out to slam her hand over his mouth. From a few feet behind her, she heard someone whisper, "Hey!" Both

181

she and Marcus spun to see where the voice had come from. Azumi shone her flashlight at a nearby tree. Behind the thick trunk, a vaguely human shape seemed to watch her.

"Poppy? Dash? Is that you?" Azumi asked.

"Just get over here," said the voice, louder this time. It was Dash. "Hurry!"

From somewhere deeper in the shadows, there came the sound of footsteps crunching through fallen leaves and pieces of glass. Shivers prickled across Azumi's skin.

They were completely exposed. She switched off her phone's light and then poked Marcus in the chest. "Yelling? Really? C'mon. Before it gets here." Then she poked him again, harder, frustrated.

"*It?*" Marcus echoed, brushing her hand away.

"You don't want to know."

Azumi crawled quietly toward the tree where Dash was hiding. Marcus followed at her heels. The footsteps crunched closer. A funky scent filled the air—dirt and mildew and rot. It was enough to make her gag. She covered her mouth and then slipped into the shadows across the stone path.

There, she found Dash and Poppy huddled together. Beside them was crouched another figure who was looking at her with worry—her sister.

CHAPTER 33

MORIKO RAISED HER finger to her lips.

The thing beyond the tree trunk was almost upon them. Azumi turned to find Marcus cowering behind her, covering his nose and mouth with both hands. His eyes were wide with terror, and he was trembling. His head was knocking against some leaves, making them shake and rattle.

Azumi pulled him close, away from the foliage, and hugged him. To her surprise, he stopped trembling and almost seemed to relax into her arms. *Just like a stupid baby.* The others were frozen. Azumi shut her eyes and silently recited a little *norito* that her obaasan had taught her, hoping a prayer might help.

The footfalls stopped a few feet away. The thing swiveled back and forth, searching. Its stench grew stronger, overwhelming, like the neighborhood compost piles back in Washington. All of a sudden, it lurched toward them, emitting an earsplitting screech. Its bony hand grabbed a hank of Moriko's hair and yanked her head backward. Dash stood and turned his phone's light into the corpse's face. Distracted by the glow, the figure glared at him and then growled. Azumi yelped, taking in its rotting floral dress, the torn burlap sack over its skull, its sticklike limbs, the noose hanging from its neck. Poppy let out a scream and Marcus clung to her side. "Let go of my sister!" Azumi cried out, springing forward. But the figure swiped at her, knocking Azumi back. Her heel caught on a root and she fell.

Moriko tried to swivel around and face the thing, but its grip was too tight. Poppy, Marcus, and Dash leapt on them. The force of their collision was enough to free Moriko and knock the corpse a few feet back. Moriko scrambled up the path toward Azumi. Azumi reached out for her, but the thing grabbed Moriko's foot and jerked her toward it again.

"Stop it, you disgusting *freak*!" she called out. It was too strong, Azumi knew. There was no way even the five of them could stop it. It would overcome Moriko, and then the rest of them, one by one.

From above, something squealed, high-pitched, like an

ancient, giant bird. Everyone looked up in time to catch pinpoints of light glinting off an object that was hurtling from the sky. A moment later, there was a crash, and the corpse was on the ground, spiked by the enormous piece of glass that Azumi had seen dangling from the rooftop.

The group let out a breath. Azumi scooted across the ground, not caring that she was scuffing her knees raw. She threw her arms around her sister and her cheeks grew wet as tears leaked from her eyes. "Are you okay?" Azumi whimpered.

"I've been through worse," said Moriko, shifting her head back and forth as if popping her neck into place. "How about you? Anyone hurt?"

The other three did not answer. They were all staring at the mess that the glass had made of the corpse. Marcus whispered, "That was . . . really . . . really . . . *really* close."

"I can't look," said Poppy, turning away. Dash followed her several yards up the path.

"Wait, Azumi," said Marcus. "This is your *sister*?"

"Yes!" she cried out, before slapping her hand over her mouth and looking over her shoulder, worried about attracting another dead thing. "I kept telling you guys she was here, waiting for us to come back," she went on quietly. Azumi turned to Moriko again. "You have no idea what we went through." She glanced down at the body lying on the path surrounded by glimmering glass. "Well, maybe you do," she said. "I feel like I'm losing my mind. I think we all do." Azumi's chest heaved as she tried to catch her breath. "Please, Moriko, can you just get us out of here?"

Moriko took Azumi's hands and held them in her lap. "I said I would. And I will." She glanced at the others and then raised an eyebrow. "And if your friends can all remember how to be very, very quiet, I might even get them out in one piece." Poppy and Dash nodded sheepishly. Marcus only stared at her as if in awe. "Where's your brother?" Moriko asked Dash. "Didn't you find him?"

"He . . . He wouldn't . . ." Dash choked, unable to finish, then clenched his fists and stared at the ground.

Moriko sighed and nodded. "Don't worry, Dash," she said, her voice soft. "Later. There's always hope." She turned to the others. "Follow me. And watch out for any more falling glass."

A warm breeze arose as they walked, rustling the leaves and bringing more of that horrible smell from somewhere deeper in the woods. Poppy and Marcus glanced at each other, remembering the hallway that had led to the rotunda and the classroom. "If this stench is any indication, I think we're definitely heading the right way," he said. But Poppy turned away, as if not wanting anything to do with him anymore. Marcus hung his head and watched the ground, not wanting to fall.

They walked and walked, stopping every now and again to hide whenever they heard scuffling from the brush.

Poppy couldn't get Cyrus out of her mind. He had tried to help rescue Esme. And she hoped that giving him the journal like Connie had told her had freed him—he'd looked peaceful for just a moment, before he fell. She *hoped* it had fixed something. It felt good, if only for a moment, to imagine that the only family she knew wasn't actually a group of monsters, even if they *were* ghosts.

Poppy kept her eyes on Moriko and Azumi, who were a few yards ahead. Marcus shuffled forward, moving toward the sisters, but Dash hung back, limping along beside Poppy.

"I can't believe Dylan tried to *kill* me." After a moment, Dash sniffed. "No, maybe I can. Maybe I deserved it."

"Of course you didn't deserve it," Poppy whispered. "Don't be silly."

"Do you think I should still track him down and try to

reason with him?" asked Dash. "Moriko said there's always hope."

"We'll find a way," said Poppy, nodding. "Dylan is just like all the other puzzles in this house. There has to be a solution. I'm sure of it."

Marcus followed a few steps behind Azumi and her sister, watching them hold hands. He thought of his own sister back in Ohio. He hoped he'd see her again soon. He wanted to race through the front door of their small house and hug his brothers. He wanted to apologize to his mother—for what, he wasn't really sure. For leaving. For reminding her of his uncle Shane. For not telling her about the music that had continued to run through his brain even after he'd promised her it had gone away. But especially, for being the worst of this group— the five who'd been called to this vile place.

He thought of his cello—his soul, his voice—lying in the foyer where everyone had dropped their luggage. *I should have gone back for it*, he told himself. *I could have tried to play some of Uncle Shane's music and protected us all. Maybe Esme wouldn't have been able to trick us. To trick* me.

He stared at Azumi's back, her shorn hair brushing her neck. Shame burned in his gut for not having seen the truth.

He'd been trying to beat Cyrus at his own game, but he'd placed his bet on the wrong girl. How could she have helped him when he'd fallen? How could she stand to be near him? How could any of them?

Marcus choked down a sense of nausea and kept walking, watching for roots and rocks that might reach up from the ground and try to trip him. To comfort himself, he hummed his uncle's melody softly for the first time in hours.

Little by little, the landscape changed. The ground grew flat. The trees spread out. The putrid breeze let up and then went away completely. Soon, the group found that they were walking on brick pavers. On either side of the path there were manicured flowers and little trimmed trees and hedges. Silver starlight frosted the edges of everything.

Azumi looked up and realized that they were strolling through the garden just outside the walls of Larkspur. Behind her, the glass walls of the greenhouse rose up several stories. And overhead was the night sky, sharp and clear and filled with a beauty that shocked her. She turned to Moriko, her mouth open in surprise. "You did it! You got us out!"

The others rushed up the path behind them. Poppy nearly knocked Moriko over with a hug. Marcus tapped Azumi's foot and smiled. Amazingly, she found herself smiling back. Dash turned and stared at the house and the tower that seemed to loom over them, as if trying to catch a glimpse of his brother up on the roof.

Moriko waved for everyone to follow her. "Let's go," she said, stepping off the path into the tall grass of the meadow. "We're still not entirely safe."

A voice called out from behind them, clear as an alarm bell. "No, you most certainly are not." And then Cyrus emerged from the shadows.

CHAPTER 34

"**GET BEHIND ME!**" Moriko shouted. "Quickly!"

But Cyrus held up his arms and yelled out, "*N-nobody move! Not if you w-wish to live!*"

The group froze, uncertain what to do. Poppy felt a strange pull in her stomach toward him, and she immediately wanted to slap herself for it. Here he was, blocking their path. Of course he'd never let them go. How could she have allowed herself to believe that he'd had a single ounce of goodness inside him? He was a liar, a monster.

In one hand, Cyrus was holding an object that glinted in the starlight. Poppy recognized it. It was the glass vial that had dropped to the floor when Esme's costume had turned to dust.

He must have picked it up. Cloudy liquid sloshed around inside it.

Moriko seemed to shrink back at the sight of it. "What are you going to do with that?" she asked him. Cyrus moved his thumb and the cork popped off the top of the vial. "Stop it!" Moriko cried out. "Leave us alone!"

"What is that?" Azumi asked her sister. "What's he holding?"

Marcus stepped forward, shaking with anger. "It's something you don't want to touch." Azumi reached out and tried to pull him back, but his jacket slipped through her fingers.

"I told you to t-trust me." Cyrus shook his head. "I wanted to help you. But you've ended up in the clutches of this . . . this *thing*!"

"Don't you call her that," Azumi shouted, jaw quivering. "She's my sister!"

"That is not your s-sister." Cyrus raised the vial over his head. "*That* is the monster that makes this place what it is. *That* is the creature that builds the illusions you see all around us. *That* is the entity that locked me in the tower. *That* is the animal that crept inside my head and twisted my thoughts and made me believe that the only way to save the children in my care was to lock the doors and light a flame. Poppy, *that* is the monster that has long stalked our family. The thing that caused your poor mother to leave you. She thought she could keep you safe."

"My mother? What are you talking about?" Poppy cried out.

"It is the thing that feeds on your fear," he went on. "It is what controls the Specials . . . and *all* the ghosts of this estate. It used to control me too! It is the house and the land and the air and the spray off of the river. *It is L-Larkspur itself.*"

"He's lying!" cried Moriko. "Don't let him twist you any further. What he's saying doesn't make any sense!"

"You have followed it to the edge of your doom," said Cyrus, speaking over her. "But I can still help you. You gave me my journal back, and it's made me stronger than I've been in decades. I can help you undo all the horrible things it has done. You've solved so many of its puzzles, Poppy. You can solve the rest. You can free the rest—"

"No more puzzles!" cried Marcus, putting himself directly between Cyrus and Moriko, who was backing slowly into the meadow with Azumi. "There's something *seriously* wrong with you!"

"No, there's not," said Cyrus, taking another step toward the group. "N-not anymore. Now I can see. I can recognize the disguises of the Beast. It's easy, actually. Azumi, haven't you n-noticed its eyes? Since when did your sister have *golden* irises?"

The group turned to look. When Moriko blinked, her eyes glinted gold even in the dim light. She shook her head. "Don't listen," she said, glancing at each of them. "He'll turn you against one another. It's another trap. *I* am your path out of here."

"But what about her eyes, Azumi?" asked Poppy. "Is Cyrus right?"

"They're brown," answered Azumi, staring at Moriko, not wanting to believe. "At least . . . they used to be."

"You don't understand," said Moriko, speaking quickly. "This isn't my real body, Azumi. It's my spirit. Things *change* afterward. Now, please. Stop listening to him. We've got to run!"

She turned, tugging Azumi's arm, but Marcus stepped toward Cyrus, reaching into his pocket. "No. I'm tired of games. I'm tired of trying to figure out who's on which side." He held up his hand, clutching the other vial with larkspur poison inside that he and Esme had stolen from the tower. "Before she went away, Esme told us not to trust anyone. Not even ourselves."

"Marcus," said Cyrus, "you don't know what you're doing."

Marcus twisted the cork away and tossed it into the grass.

"Wait!" said Poppy. "What if Cyrus is right?"

But Marcus whipped the vial forward anyway, splashing the liquid into the old man's face.

CHAPTER 35

CYRUS'S SHRIEKS PIERCED the night. He threw his hands to his face and then dropped to the ground, crying in agony. Hissing smoke rose up from his body in the grass.

"What did you do?" shouted Poppy.

"I saved us!" said Marcus. Turning to Azumi and Moriko, he added, "Come on! Let's go!"

The sisters started to run down the slight slope, toward the dark line of trees ahead. Marcus, Dash, and Poppy followed a short distance behind them. The trees seemed to rise up as they got closer. The wind howled through the branches deep in the woods, making them sway and dance in the dark.

Ahead, Azumi and Moriko paused at the edge of the forest,

waiting for the others to catch up. "Hold on, we can't go in there," said Dash, limping behind them. "We'll get lost."

"We have to find the driveway," Poppy agreed. "It's the only way back to the gate."

"What we need to do is get out of the open," said Moriko, glancing back up the hill. The house stood like a Gothic fortress, glaring down at them. "Cyrus could be coming for us right now."

"But we're not going to just follow you into the woods!" said Dash. "Not after—"

"You still don't believe her?" Azumi asked, incredulous. "She got us out of Larkspur! That's more than we can say for *good old* Cyrus. Marcus was right. That blue goop stopped the old man in his tracks."

"But what if *Cyrus* was right?" Poppy insisted, her soft voice raised to a shriek. "He knew things about my family. About my mother! I want to know more!"

Moriko sighed. "Poppy . . ."

Marcus couldn't listen anymore. Too many games. Too many sides. His head felt fuzzy, and it was impossible to focus. He hadn't felt clear since he'd sat down to play with his uncle Shane, back in the music room.

He closed his eyes and began to hum, just a couple of bars

of the music he'd heard when he first arrived at Larkspur, before all the games and horror had started.

"Don't," said Moriko.

Everyone turned toward her. The night grew very quiet.

"What's wrong?" asked Azumi, her voice suddenly small.

Marcus heard the soft melody again, just a whisper of it on the wind, and for a moment he felt warm, like Uncle Shane was reaching out to protect him one more time. He pursed his lips, whistling the tune, and the music seemed to bounce around the group, heading up the hill and down into the woods.

Moriko grabbed her stomach and then hunched over, tossing her blue hair over her face. "I-it hurts!" she stammered. "Please! Stop!"

Marcus broke off for a moment, watching her struggle and squirm, but he couldn't bring himself to stop humming his uncle's tune.

"Marcus," said Azumi, worry rising in her voice, "maybe this isn't a good idea—"

Moriko released a shrieking, gurgling sort of howl, as if a thousand predators were crying out in anger and pain.

Marcus choked and lost the melody.

The group stepped even farther away from Moriko, and she whipped her head up. Her appearance had changed. Her skin was swelling, her face growing puffy and purple as if filling with fluid, and soon her eyes' golden glow winked out. She shook as if she were in agony, unable to express it aloud through her inflamed lips, which were now splitting, the skin cracking open, torrents of blue liquid dripping down her chin and neck.

"Moriko!" Azumi cried out, reaching toward her trembling sister. "What's happening to you?"

"Azumi, stay back!" said Dash.

"Marcus, don't stop," Poppy whispered.

Moriko shuddered, wrenching her spine backward at an impossible angle, and growing taller. Her bruised, stretched skin broke and then sloughed to the ground. A wet puddle in the grass.

Too frightened to move, or even scream, Poppy, Dash, and Azumi clung to one another as the Beast rose to its full height. They craned their necks to stare in awe at a body that appeared to be made of millions of bones and branches tied together with blackened sinew and trapped within a dark, gauzy skin.

Squeezing his eyes closed, Marcus only hummed louder.

Poppy cried out, "Marcus, stop! You're making it mad!"

Marcus opened his eyes, and what he saw standing at the

edge of the forest stole his voice from his chest. His mouth dropped open and his tongue clicked quietly.

"You guys, you have to run!" he finally gasped. "I think I can hold it off."

"What about—" Poppy started, but Marcus called over her.

"My uncle will protect me!"

Poppy looked at the creature, even as Dash tugged her arm. Two golden flames were alight deep inside a long, equine skull, glaring down at them with fury. A heavy jaw seemed to unlatch, widening as the thing let out a deafening roar. Hundreds of long, skinny teeth protruded, threatening to tear open the casing of its own face.

"Do what Cyrus said! RUN!" Marcus shoved Poppy toward Azumi, then started humming even louder, turning to face the shadow creature. Dash and Azumi dragged Poppy away fast as they could.

Dash felt numb, unable to even feel his legs carrying him through the grass. He turned, and faster than he could see, the Beast swung out a long skinny arm, sending Marcus flying toward the line of trees. A disturbing crunch rang out as he hit a thick trunk before dropping to the ground several feet below. Poppy and Azumi whipped around.

"No!!" Azumi shrieked.

But the Beast stalked slowly toward the small, dark shape that was Marcus, a monstrous cat playing with its prey.

"GO!" Poppy choked out, and they turned and fled.

It felt as though someone had taken a blunt soup spoon and scooped out Azumi's insides. Her lungs didn't want to work anymore. It felt like the air was too heavy to pull in. Blips of thought passed through her head, but she seemed unable to capture any of it.

Marcus?

Psychic . . . break . . . ?

Shadow . . . Beast . . . ?

Moriko?

Where . . . am . . . I?

Then, in the distance, there came another ground-shaking roar. Poppy and Dash pushed faster, but Azumi collapsed, unable to continue. She clasped her thighs against her chest.

"Come on, Azumi!" cried Dash, going back and pulling at her arm, leading her into the brush at the edge of the woods. "We've got to hide." When she wouldn't move, Poppy helped Dash carry her out of the meadow. Soon, they all ducked into the thick bushes in the darkness.

You're still at Larkspur, said a voice in her head. It sounded like Moriko. The *real* Moriko—as if she were actually there with her. *You need to leave. Listen to what the man said: You have to set them free!* This wasn't really happening, was it? It had to be a dream. Sleepwalking again. The world all around her felt so *unreal.* Then Dash brushed against her arm and she began to sense other things—the warm night breeze, the grass tickling her calves, the tightness of her face where her tears were beginning to dry—detailed and tactile moments that she never experienced while dreaming.

Through the branches, they could make out the large silhouette of the creature, hovering around the spot where Marcus had fallen. Suddenly, as if it caught a whiff of something off in the woods, it turned and shuffled into the brush, crunching saplings and stomping fallen branches as it pursued its new target.

Azumi cried out.

Dash grabbed her hand and pulled her toward him. "Azumi, we have to be quiet. That thing is still listening."

"We've got to go to him," said Poppy. "He's probably hurt really bad."

Slowly, they edged back toward the place where Marcus was lying on his side, his legs bent backward, his arms

stretched over his head. His face was tilted down, and none of them could see if his eyes were open or closed.

Poppy knelt and then hitched a breath. "I-I think . . . I think he's gone."

Dash crossed his arms and stepped away before turning to face the house. He shook his head slightly, as if he'd already known the truth, and it was finally sinking in.

"It's my fault," Azumi whispered. Marcus had hurt her. He'd betrayed her. But he didn't deserve this. Nobody did. "I didn't know—"

"It's nobody's fault," said Poppy, grabbing Azumi, enclosing her in her arms.

"You don't understand," said Azumi, her voice muffled in Poppy's T-shirt. "If I hadn't trusted her . . . I thought she was my sister. I *needed* her to be my sister."

"*It's nobody's fault*," Poppy repeated, her voice harder this time.

The girls fell silent as they hugged each other. Dash sat beside them, staring up at the night sky.

"We have to start moving," he said finally, refusing to look at Marcus. A flurry of memories lit through him. Dylan's body was clear in his mind, lying on the floor of the dressing room and then on the floor in the tower room. Cyrus collapsing into the grass. Marcus flying through the air and landing, so still. Dash shook his head, straightening his spine. "We have to find the driveway and the path through the woods to the gate. We need to find the real way out."

Poppy nodded. "That thing will come back. I know it."

"Which way do we go?" asked Azumi, her teeth chattering.

Dash pointed toward the dark and sprawling mansion. His arm felt heavy. Lifeless. "The path's on the other side of the hill. On the other side of the house."

"There's no way I'm going near that place," said Azumi.

"Then we'll go around," said Poppy. "We'll stay near the line of trees, but far enough from the shadows so that we can see what's coming."

"We'll never be able to see what's coming," said Dash.

Azumi and Poppy glanced down at Marcus. "Should we try . . . should we take him with us?" asked Azumi.

Dash sniffed. "We can't. We might not even make it by ourselves."

"We're going to make it," said Poppy. "We've already gotten out of the house. It's only a little bit farther now."

"What about your brother, Dash?" asked Azumi. "You're going to leave him here too?"

Dash's spine slumped. Dizzy, he placed his palms over his eyes, scrubbing at them to hold in tears. "I don't even know where to start looking," he said. "I-I can't go back into that building again. Not after what we just saw."

"And if we do find him," said Azumi, "how can we be sure it's really him?"

"You're both right," Poppy whispered. "You have to save *you*, Dash. Dylan—the real Dylan—would have wanted that. Right?"

After a moment, Dash nodded. Slowly, he brought himself to his feet. "We have to leave him behind." Reaching down, he helped the girls stand up too.

They waited another moment. Poppy thought of Marcus, hoping that he was safe now. Dreaming of his cello, of his uncle, of their melody. Silently, each of them thanked him for being brave, for the gift of his song, even when he must have feared what it would cost. Then, holding hands, they stepped back into the meadow's tall grass and headed along the line of trees, straddling both the light from the stars and the forest's overreaching shadow.

CHAPTER 36

IN A DARK place in the woods, not far from where Marcus's body is lying, Dylan watches his brother head off with the two girls. He steps forward into the wide furrow of earth that the creature left in its wake as it dragged itself away.

A spot just below one of his eyes is twitching, but when Dylan tries to scratch it, his finger bumps into the thick plastic mask that he cannot remove. The twitch grows more uncomfortable as Dash walks along the edge of the forest. It's so bad that Dylan wants to shout and thrash, to throw himself onto the ground and pound his fists into the dirt. But he can't scream. He can't do any of the things he wants to do. Something won't let him.

Back in the tower, as that same something moved his body

around like a puppet, he'd begged for his brother's help. *My mask is stuck. Take it off me, Dash. Take it off! Fix me . . . I need you, little brother.* But Dash had fought him instead, like when they were little and one of them wouldn't share a favorite toy.

And now his brother is walking away. Dash is leaving him alone here in this nightmare place, just like the selfish jerk that Dylan has always suspected lurked underneath his brother's skin.

Don't let him go, says a voice in Dylan's head. It sounds like Del, the producer. Or maybe like Cyrus, the director. Or maybe like the thing that had been hiding inside Azumi's sister. All of the voices combine and then add, *Make him pay for what he's done.*

"We'll help you."

Dylan discovers that he's not alone after all. The other members of the cast have found him. Only three of them left now. The girl in the cat mask and the boys in the bear and rabbit masks stroll quietly through the brush behind him, approaching calmly. As if this is only a scene in a story, a movie, a dream. And they are only doing their jobs.

"We lost our families too," says the girl in the cat mask. It sounds like she's reading from a script, telling the beginning of a bedtime story. She's very convincing. Dylan finds comfort in her words. "A long time ago. But we found one another." Her mask shifts, the mouth twisting into a wicked smile. "And now we have you."

Together, the four masked children turn back toward the meadow, searching through the silhouettes of tree trunks for the place where Poppy, Azumi, and Dash have disappeared into the distance.

Silently, they follow.

ART CREDITS

ENDPAPERS
Photos ©: 2–3: background illustration: Larry Rostant for Scholastic; 4: fire: CG Textures; 4–5: wallpaper: clearviewstock/Shutterstock, Inc.; 6–7: Shadow House illustration: Shane Rebenschied for Scholastic; Shadow House mansion: Dariush M/Shutterstock, Inc., Shadow House fog: Maxim van Asseldonk/Shutterstock, Inc., Shadow House clouds: Aon_Skynotlimit/Shutterstock, Inc., foreground grass and trees: Maxim van Asseldonk/Shutterstock, Inc.

INTERIOR
Photos ©: cover background illustration: Larry Rostant for Scholastic; 18: couple: Joey Boylan/Getty Images, man suit and hat: ysbrandcosijn/Fotolia, lady hat: Alexey Yuzhakov/Shutterstock, Inc., doorway and background: Kochneva Tetyana/Shutterstock, Inc., skull: Lukas Gojda/Fotolia; 44–45: greenhouse: Patrik Stedrak/Fotolia, bench: KateD/Fotolia, hanging legs: Everett Collection/Shutterstock, Inc., leaves: keantian/Fotolia, Monkey Focus/Shutterstock, Inc., photobee/Fotolia; 51: classroom: Sami Sert/Getty Images, chalkboard: urfin/Shutterstock, Inc., cat mask: CSA Plastock/Getty Images; 59: water: spectrumx86/Fotolia; arms: prudkov/Fotolia, piranka/Getty Images, russal/Shutterstock, Inc., Anton Sokolov/Fotolia, body: Blake Sinclair/Getty Images; 83: hallway: phoelixDE/Shutterstock, Inc., mask: vaij/Fotolia, boy illustration: Larry Rostant for Scholastic; 103: rabbit: Rubberball/Mike Kemp/Getty Images; fox: nullplus/Getty Images; bobcat: eastmanphoto/Fotolia; window: littleny/Fotolia; bookshelf: dmitrygolikov/Fotolia; 128: drawers set: carl ballou/Shutterstock, Inc.; hanging shoe: Marie Charouzova/Shutterstock, Inc.; shoes: Rainer Fuhrmann/Shutterstock, Inc. and Taborsky/Shutterstock, Inc.; candy: philip kinsey/Fotolia; books: Paul Orr/Shutterstock, Inc.; folders: Valentin Agapov/Shutterstock, Inc.; files: Szasz-Fabian Erika/Fotolia; doll: unclepepin/Shutterstock, Inc.; football: spxChrome/Getty Images; sheet music: Nikolai Sorokin/Fotolia; 138: falling man illustration: Erika Scipione for Scholastic; frame: smuay/Fotolia; wallpaper: Vadelma/Shutterstock, Inc.; frame: CG Textures; 192: Shadow House illustration: Shane Rebenschied for Scholastic, Shadow House mansion: Dariush M/Shutterstock, Inc., Shadow House fog: Maxim van Asseldonk/Shutterstock, Inc., Shadow House clouds: Aon_Skynotlimit/Shutterstock, Inc., Shadow House moon: Mykola

About the Author

Dan Poblocki is the author of several books for young readers, including *The House on Stone's Throw Island*, *The Book of Bad Things*, *The Nightmarys*, *The Stone Child*, and the Mysterious Four series. His recent novels, *The Ghost of Graylock* and *The Haunting of Gabriel Ashe*, were both Junior Library Guild selections and made the American Library Association's Best Fiction for Young Adults list in 2013 and 2014. Dan lives in Brooklyn and often writes in a cafe filled with specimen jars, taxidermied animals, and stacks of old books. Visit him online at www.danpoblocki.com.

Discover Your Spirit Animal!

THE CAHILLS ARE BACK...
WITH A VENGEANCE!

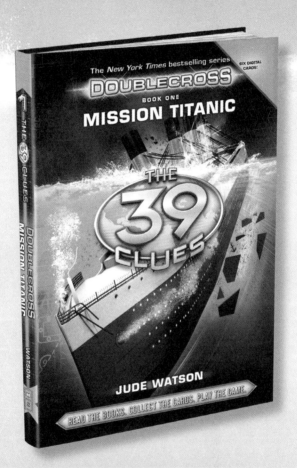

Dan and Amy reunited the powerful Cahill family and ushered in a new era of peace. Or so they thought. But not every Cahill is ready to kiss and make up. And the mayhem they unleash will be nothing like you've seen before...

Read the Book. Play the Game.

BOOK 3

SHADOW HOUSE

Poppy, Dash, Azumi, and Dylan may have made it out of
Shadow House—but the grounds are a whole new nightmare. Someone they thought was a friend is hunting them,
and there's no place that's safe now that they've woken
the shadow creature.

   If they want to survive, they'll have to figure out once
and for all what the house wants from them, and what—or
who—they'll need to leave behind in order to escape . . .
or risk being trapped within Shadow House forever.

Step into Shadow House.

Enter Shadow House

Each image in the
book reveals a
haunting in the app.

Search out hidden
sigils in the book
for bonus scares in
the app.

Step into ghost stories,
where the choices you make
determine your fate.

CAN YOU ESCAPE?